SONS OF

WUNDURIA

BY JOSHUA ALLEN

To Kelly,

Thankyou

[signature]

ISBN 979-8-9918954-1-5
PRINT
1st Edition Revised Paperback

For Additional Resources:
www.instagram.com/sonsofwunduria/
www.SonsOfWunduria.com
BV Design - Insta @bv_design_

- WUNDURIA -

Within the splendor of Earth is a most secluded place where tall trees grow and animals of all sorts graze. A place you can live a day, then turn away or linger if you wish. This is where Wunduria exists.

No one knows where it is on a map, although it must be somewhere. Wunduria escapes our maps and understanding, so instead of finding it, imagine a place where the oceans find peace, where the seas protect a secret. A place that eludes all search and comprehension, where reality dares not venture.

This island is a home for the extraordinary. It's a place untouched by harsh realities, a relic that has slipped through the cracks of time. Its inhabitants are blissfully unaware of any existence beyond their island paradise. They are the fortunate ones, living in a world of their own.

But things are changing...

Chapter 1: A Tree Home

A tree is a lovely place to make a home, no matter how odd it may seem. One might wonder why a person would choose such a place to live. "For the love of natural quaintness," Haven would tell those who asked.

"But how is this achieved?" One wondered.

To which Haven replied, "With patience and care."

One day, while shepherding the King's sheep, Haven June, a young lad, searched for a lamb that strayed from the flock. Inside the aperture of a large oak, he found the lamb seeking shade from the sun. He crawled in there to cuddle the whimpering thing. When inside, to his surprise, he found it quite roomy. With the lamb in his arms, he deemed the place comfortable. It offered relief and relaxation.

It occurred to him at that moment that while finding a lost sheep, he found a place he so very much cherished. Shepherding was, in itself, a reward.

He crawled in there many times and sat, mesmerized by the comfort it provided. He deemed the place unexplainable. Despite the tree's hollowed-out bottom, it stood sturdy with life, even prospering more than all the other trees.

Haven camped in it one night, and before falling asleep, he considered expanding the room. The following day, he felt refreshed, glowing with contentment. "Yes, I will make this my home," he said.

He began by brushing and clearing the floor until it was soft. Eventually, he increased the room's height so he could stand without bumping his head. He sculpted a place of artistry, combining nature's essence with his craftsmanship. He did so carefully to avoid harming the tree.

After several years, he found it adequate to fit a bed, end table, and shelves. After further furnishing it with a door and window, he considered it a home he could live in—a place of peace and comfort.

Outside the door lay moss-laden stones. He would sit there on his steps and read. The ancient sentinels of the woods were before him, and a creek flowed quietly just a few steps away. He had made a home and a harmonious union of himself and woodland. He called it his Tree Home.

By this time, he had grown tall and well-framed. Despite his growth, his tree home still suited him. It fit his comforts, providing him with solitude. He built a tiny stove to make coffee, tea, and soup. There was also a nook he carved into a wall. It became more of a pantry than anything else.

His mother minded little that he left to live alone in a tree out near the woods. He wasn't far away, and the king approved the whole matter, seeing that the tree existed on the rear portion of the royal villa's estate. He knew it to be peaceful back there and a place of safety.

One could find trails there that led to resting places. After returning the sheep to their sheepfold, Haven would randomly pick a trail and wander down it until he was deep into the dense forest, conversing with the earth itself. The rustle of leaves and chirping birds became the voice that spoke back to him, soothing his soul. Such pleasantness rested in his heart there. He loved it so much he'd take his loyal friend, Thunder, a stallion from the wild.

Years prior, when Haven entered his adolescence, he came face to face with the horse. Initially, the encounters were brief, filled with caution and curiosity from both. Yet, as days passed into weeks, a silent understanding wove between them, a mutual respect born from shared moments in the vast open fields.

With a grace that didn't match his human form, Haven displayed a fantastic ability to run across grassy stretches with a speed that nearly matched the stallion's. Of course, Thunder would eventually outrun him by great lengths. But Haven's speed fascinated the horse. It enjoyed racing with its human friend.

Haven mounted the stallion without saddle or bridle, an act that, to any onlooker, would have seemed a foolhardy act of fun. Yet there was no bucking, no fierce resistance by the stallion, only an act of acceptance. Together, they moved as one entity across the landscape. He commanded the animal with gentle pressures of his knees and weight shifts, with whispers and soft touch. Young man and animal, chasing the wind with a language only they understood.

Under the endless blue sky, they spent many afternoons capturing the feeling of freedom. There, bound by an invisible thread of companionship, Thunder kept Haven busy with a grateful heart. The land was so serene Haven would often daydream there. It was very noticeable when he did this. Thunder would nudge him on the side with its snout, reminding him there was a home to return to.

At eighteen years of age, Haven's daydreams grew more frequent. He knew it, too, but felt his musings to be necessary. It was time to find his place in Wunduria. He had plenty of reason to fixate on his future and the sort of man he wanted to become.

While sitting by a crackling campfire one evening, he reflected on his journey from boyhood to eventual adulthood. *What is next for me?*

He lifted his head, looking up at the stars. There were so many to see; it impressed him they were so far out of reach. Despite their beauty, he lowered his head and, for once, was uninterested in the spectacle. He shut his eyes, listened to the sounds of the night, and exhaled deeply. *Who am I to become? What is my greater purpose? I want to be more.*

~ ~ ~

Mornings have a flair for renewing one's sensibilities. Haven sipped his coffee, content being the shepherd for the royal household. During his customary morning walk, Thunder, his loyal companion, trotted alongside, eagerly munching on every carrot offered. The gentle sound of Thunder's neighs and the rhythmic swish of its tail never failed to bring a smile to Haven's face. "You're having a good time, aren't you, boy?" He said, his voice filled with affection, as he patted Thunder's side.

After Thunder had finished all the carrots, it trotted off towards the fields, its usual place to spend the day. Haven, feeling a sudden urgency, quickened his pace towards the royal family's villa. There, his mother, in a hurried and unexpected farewell, departed on a trip with the queen. It was a last-minute decision that the queen had given her no option to refuse.

"I love you, dear!" His mother exclaimed, blowing him a kiss. "Be safe and be happy!"

He blew a kiss in kind and watched their carriage disappear down the road. He knew he'd feel both their absences. They were incredible influences for him.

King Mikel Aku approached, wearing his morning attire. Haven noticed his stride to be much more casual than usual. His dark skin shined in the sunlight. His eyes, deep and dark, sparkled with a boyish glee that belied his age.

Despite the vastness between their worlds, they shared a unique bond of friendship that transcended their roles as king and servant. Though they were very different, they found solace in one another's company. They shared a common philosophy: work hard and savor the fruits of one's labor.

"They're off to experience the greatness of the black sand beaches of Zyra." King Aku said.

Haven bowed slightly, exchanging smiles with the king. "Yes, your Majesty, my mother appreciates your gift. She loves to be by the water."

"I hope she enjoys it," he said graciously. "Haven," he continued, his voice carrying authority but with the warmth of concern. "The days of tending to sheep are behind you. It is time you become your own man, away from the comforts of home."

Haven inhaled deeply as he knew of the king's high expectations for him. He just hadn't expected this conversation so soon. He struggled to envision the future laid out before him. His path from young shepherd to adulthood was unclear.

"My king," he stuttered, looking away. "I am humbled by your confidence in me, but I must confess, the thought of leaving behind all I know fills me with great apprehension," he admitted with an unsteady voice. "I trust your wisdom, but I do not trust mine."

"So these anxieties consume you? Young men doubt what they do not see. What they have not lived," the King replied. "But do not fear; doubts are common among youngsters. Just understand your future isn't in your tree home; it's out there in the unknown. It's time you face challenges that chisel away your youthful exterior."

After a huff, Haven replied quietly. "I know, my king."

A gentle grin rose to Mikel Aku's face. "Life will hand you many difficult choices; the consequences of your mistakes often outweigh your successes. But do not let that consume you. A man is built upon hardships."

Haven mustered a grimacing nod, acknowledging the king's words.

"You are prepared to meet those challenges, my young friend," the king said assuredly. "Haven June, today I relieve you of your duties as my flock's shepherd. You must decide what sort of man you are to be. Go, spend the day freely, explore my kingdom, and find what fulfills your heart. May it lead you one step closer to your future self."

"Yes, my king," he replied quietly. But as he turned away, the king added another jab of uncertainty.

"When you return, expect the unexpected," the king said. "Adulthood is full of it." After that, he left Haven alone to fulfill his kingly obligations.

Haven felt the pressure to face the future, so he lingered in thought, wandering the royal grounds.

His musings ended as he entered a wide field of red dandelion. Out in the distance, a hearty neigh echoed across the field. Haven scanned over the landscape. His gaze, keen as a falcon's, scanned the verdant expanse before him. Like a clarion call, he whistled into the great wide yonder, summoning his stalwart steed. In a flurry of hooves and a cascade of dirt, the noble beast appeared, a creature of grace and strength.

So he charged the animal. With a deft leap, he mounted Thunder, stationing himself on the horse's back. They galloped into the immense plains beyond their home, bound by the timeless allure of adventure.

Together, they found peace riding through San Hadza's calm places. They explored green meadows and visited brooks. Thunder grazed upon lush grass pastures, and Haven found berries to snack on. They watched a vixen fox play with its cubs. Then he saw quiet things like rabbits lying among a patch of lupine. As they hopped around wildflowers, Thunder mimicked their fun.

Beyond there, they rested on a patch of moss at the bottom of a hill. They listened to songbirds and buzzing things with tiny wings near a thicket of bushes and small trees.

By dusk, they had returned home without a care. Haven's peace had returned to him, though he had given little thought to his future.

A TREE HOME

At nightfall, Thunder slept under a lean-to Haven built for him some time ago. After saying goodnight, he stepped inside his tree home, ready to sleep. A slight breeze came through an open window, which cooled his skin, refreshing him.

In the night's quietness, with only the moon's silver light seeping through the window, he stood before a mirror, inspecting his appearance. He removed his tunic and flexed. His frame lacked the ruggedness and strength of a man. A bitter thought came to his mind: *I am no longer a shepherd boy.*

Looking around the room at his things, he found them shrouded in shadows. He felt uneasy inside his tree home, which he built for comfort. How long will this be my home? What am I to do with all my tomorrows?

He lit a candle; its flame flickered to life, lighting the tiny room. He leaned closer to the mirror. His blue eyes, deep pools of thought, searched his reflection for answers. The candlelight danced across his features, highlighting the contours of his face. He watched the shadows play along his sharp jawline and through the tousles of his brown hair. Who will I become?

For the first time, he scrutinized his reflection, finding an unwelcome softness in his handsomeness. The gentle light stressed the tenderness of his face. He touched it and brushed his hand over his cheek, bothered by its unmarked smoothness. *I'm not a man yet.*

He opened a drawer from his nightstand and pulled out a knife. Like so many times before, his imagination transformed the quiet room into a tumultuous battlefield. He gripped the knife tighter, a smaller substitute for the deadly steel of a warrior's sword, and swung it through the air, defending a lethal strike. His stance widened, rooted, and formidable as he embodied the heart of a mighty warrior. His eyes fixed on the fire of battle. The soft glow of the candle cast long, heroic shadows against the walls as he pretended to fight enemies from legends long ago.

His face contorted with the intensity of the imaginary fight, a fierce grimace replacing the youthful softness. He flung the blade into the door. It pierced the wood. He stood victorious on the battlefield of his mind's eye, marked by battle scars. *I am a hero.*

But in the loneliness of his home, he sat on the edge of his mattress, knowing it was all for naught. There, his imagined battle faded into the silence. He stared at the blade, now just a tool that enabled a fantasy. He let out a deep, steady breath, feeling reality settle back upon his shoulders.

He then pulled the blade from the door and placed it back into his nightstand, leaving the drawer open, hoping to be inspired again. In the quiet aftermath of his imagined heroics, he confronted the reality of his life: he knew the life of a shepherd rather than a victorious hero.

He grew pensive there in a flickering shadow but found solace in the thought that perhaps true courage lies in embracing who he is and in his foundational belief, which he had held for many years: peace is its own victory.

Something caught his attention as he dropped to his bed. In the drawer behind the knife, he spotted a keepsake. He sat up and stared at it, feeling it waiting for retrieval. So he removed the keepsake from its hiding place.

It was a necklace made from a simple cable chain. A round, hardened green resin pendant hung from it. It was a gift from his father, given to him many years prior, a tangible connection to the man he had not seen since his early childhood.

His glance returned to his reflection in the mirror. As he fastened the necklace around his neck, a surprising surge of confidence washed over him. The metal felt cold against his skin, but the sensation it brought was warm, and a sense of pride filled him with conviction.

He held the green pendant in his right hand. A tiny capsule sat in the center. Though he hadn't forgotten the necklace's significance, he couldn't remember what the tiny capsule contained, but at that moment, it did not matter to him. He felt an inexplicable importance pulsating through the pendant as if it carried the silent promises and hopes his father had for him. It was more than just a piece of jewelry; it symbolized strength.

He straightened his posture and stood tall. Staring at his reflection, he felt an unwavering confidence. He puffed out his chest and then lifted his arms, flexing his muscles.

This necklace recalled his earliest memory of his father. Though vague, he remembered his father's words: "Always keep it."

Despite his mixed emotions for the man, Haven did just so, never losing it and wearing it occasionally. He believed it served as a reminder that he had a father out there who loved him as if his father's unseen support could guide him into his future.

"I need purpose," he whispered, alone in the golden hues of his candle-lit tree home. "But where do I find it?"

He sat at the edge of his bed, discontent, searching his mind for answers.

Just then, he heard a knock. Startled by the noise, he jerked with fright. He looked to the door with a racing heart. Another knock, this time several of them.

"Hello?" he questioned loudly, grabbing the blade once again. "Who's there?"

2
THE UNEXPECTED

Haven's heart raced as the unwelcome knocks echoed through his hollow tree home. "Who is it?" he called out, his hand gripping the blade he kept for potential dangers like this.

"It is I, the one you've never met," came an old man's voice from the other side.

Haven's eyebrows furrowed at the puzzling introduction. He mumbled, putting on pants in case he'd be obliged to open the door. "What is your name?" he asked, his voice tinged with curiosity.

"Open the door!" The old man replied, knocking aggressively.

"I will not," Haven shouted.

"You will if you do!"

Haven's face wrinkled. "I do not know who you are," he complained.

The old man's voice took on a grumpy tone. "I know! I just said you've never met me! Oh, for goodness sake, no one likes surprises anymore," he grumbled. "I am Jehu, a wise one of the Highest Council. Now, open up!"

Haven's eyebrows shot up. The chance that a Geezer stood at his doorstep was far-fetched, but if true, it meant unpredictable things. He pulled back his curtain and peered at the man, who looked the part.

The alleged Geezer had a weathered face that bore the lines of contemplation and a lifetime of learning. Deep-set eyes, twinkling with the light of ancient secrets, peered out from beneath a crinkled brow. A beard, long and white as the winter's snow, cascaded down his chest. His tattered robes, adorned with intricate symbols and sigils of arcane significance, draped loosely around his form, hinting at his ancient understanding of Wunduria's greatest mysteries.

Looking the old man up and down, Haven cautiously opened the door and found himself face to face with a whimsical old man holding a staff that brightened at the top. "Can I help you?" Haven asked, squinting.

"Good evening, young Haven!" the old man beamed, wrinkles spread across his face. "I know the hour is late, but I find twilight the best time for conversation."

"Oh, uh," Haven stammered, still uncertain if the old man was who he claimed to be.

The Geezer leaned in conspiratorially, his voice dropping to a stage whisper. "I am looking for a brave young man who can tame an earthquake."

Haven wondered what it meant to tame an earthquake.

"Are you that young man?" Jehu asked, smiling and hopeful.

Haven blinked several times, looking past the old man suspiciously. "I'm not sure if I heard you correctly. Tame an earthquake, you say?"

"Yes, indeed!" Jehu exclaimed, a mischievous glint in his eye. "I was told you're just the person for the job."

"That's strange," Haven said. "Who told—"

"Strange," the old man said with a grin. "I do like the strange things in life." A breeze passed over him at that moment, and his smell entered the tree home—an earthly scent, possibly patchouli.

"I think there might be a misunderstanding, sir," Haven responded, rubbing his nose. "I am a peaceful shepherd, not someone who can tame earthquakes if such a thing is possible."

The Geezer waved a dismissive hand. "Nonsense, my boy! You are a brave man, and it is possible! A wise man told me so. He said I'd find you living inside a tree on the king's land. And here you are."

Haven stammered again. "Who told you this?"

"Someone I trust," he answered.

"Is this about those earthquakes in the north?"

"Yes, you could say that," he replied, glancing inside Haven's tree home. "Are you going to invite me in or not?" He griped, shaking from the night's chill. "I'm a cold old man. Let me inside."

Haven stepped aside while the old man shuffled in quickly, his lively demeanor filling the small space with awkwardness. His bright staff knocked Haven on the head as he entered, eliciting a chuckled apology.

Feeling its quaintness overbearing, he immediately turned around and left the tree home. "Oh, no, no, I can't stay in this closet of yours," he protested. On his way out, his staff again hit Haven's head, prompting mumbles of complaint.

"Oh, no. Small places won't do. I can't," he grumbled again.

Rubbing his head, Haven sighed. He'd had enough of this unexpected encounter. Haven closed the door, shaking his head. "Whoever that old man is, he is not a Geezer," he muttered. But as the words left his mouth, the door swung open, and the old man's hand yanked him by the ear. Haven stumbled sideways in surprise. He whined all the way outside.

"You little brat, I am too a Geezer," he objected with a curled lip, yanking Haven outside. His outstretched arm revealed the symbols of wisdom lore tattooed on his wrist, which confirmed his Geezer identity.

He swung his staff to bop Haven's head, but this time, Haven caught it. "Not this time," Haven hissed, holding the staff tightly.

The Geezer's eyes widened. "Ah, good to see you have your wits about you." He then pointed his staff toward silhouettes in the darkness several steps away. "Now, let's see how you handle a group of delinquents."

Haven turned to several ominous silhouettes gathered around his fire pit. He squinted his eyes into the dark and counted six of them. The Geezer pushed Haven towards them.

"Who are they?" Haven asked.

"Strangers, I suppose." The Geezer replied softly—a statement giving way to intrigue.

Haven approached them cautiously. His breath grew shallow, and his stomach sank—nervousness took hold of him. The Geezer draped a cloak over Haven, one more elegant than he usually wore. The interior, lined with fur, provided warmth against his bare skin. Cooled by the night's air, his necklace still dangled from his neck, with the cold green pendant resting on his chest.

He took his position before the six figures. They stood around a small flame resting at the bottom of a woodpile. The Geezer whispered words from an ancient language few understood.

"What are you saying?" Haven asked him.

The Geezer leaned forward and replied, "I am trying to convince myself that we didn't travel all this way for nothing. Don't disappoint us." He then walked past him toward the others, bumping Haven as he did so, and dropped the gleaming top of his staff into the woodpile, igniting it into a blazing fire.

THE UNEXPECTED

Eager yet wary of who awaited him in the darkness, Haven looked around to find six young men staring back at him with their arms crossed. Three were to his right, and three were to his left. They were indeed strangers, all unique in physique and dress, their expressions full of contempt.

"There are six of them." The Geezer said to him.

"Yeah, I can count," Haven muttered. "Not sure why they're here, but I must alert the king's guards. These strangers are intruding on royal land."

The Geezer nodded toward someone walking towards them in the dark. "How about you tell the king yourself?"

Looking across the fire, Haven fixed his eyes on the approaching person. The flickering flames heightened, reaching further toward the night sky above. He watched a man step out of the darkness. Dressed in a large purple surcoat, King Aku regally entered the scene with his eyes fixed on Haven.

He addressed the young men with his signature cadence: "I have assembled you here for a most urgent matter." He then lowered his hands, signaling them to sit.

All six took their seats, giving the king their full attention. He gestured for Haven to sit as well. He did so, looking back at the king, searching for reassurance or a hint of what all this meant, but found only urgency in the king's expression as he again addressed the group.

"Youthful strangers of Wunduria, you are here to answer an evil that awakes in the north. A great purpose awaits. Wunduria's future depends upon you."

THESE YOUTHFUL STRANGERS WERE...

BLUFF

Closest to Haven, on his right, was Bluff, a Drifter from the Anthills. His brown skin, weathered by the harsh desert sun, spoke of a life spent wandering the unforgiving sands. On top of his head stood black, soft, curly hair. Its random sharp edges hinted at idle boasts of danger. He wore various armor and garbs, a patchwork of styles and materials from many tribes and kingdoms, each bearing its own story of adventure and victory. He held a red staff in his hand, its color vibrant against the muted tones of his attire, a symbol of prowess. He also wore a circlet around his forehead called an Erokan, a traditional ornament believed to protect one's thoughts. Despite the stern set of his features, there was a quiet strength in his presence that presented a uniqueness to his composure. He was a stoic one.

SVEN

Following Bluff was Sven, a diminutive Norseman dressed in traditional Viking attire. Despite his small size, he radiated a stubborn, fighter-like determination, his gaze unwavering and his grip firm on his shield and axe. His body language mirrored that of the great warriors of the Vig Norse lands, a warrior's stance that commanded respect even from the most hardened criminals.

EPOCH

After him, closest to King Aku, was a Giant Tribesman named Epoch. His head, except for a fade on top, was bare. His brown leather clothes, a mark of his Central Bush heritage, were practical and showcased his people's artistry—gauntlets wrapped around his forearms, a hint of his strength. A knife hung from his belt, though it appeared he'd instead use his fists in battle. Despite his young age, his height and thick body would surpass most.

LUNAR

Directly across the fire from the Giant sat an albino named Lunar from the land of Pulver, a forest of white trees with pale leaves. He sat there clearly skittish, looking around himself, paranoid. He held his traveling bag close to his chest, gripping it tightly. Though the fire's light made it difficult to see, his skin glowed a soft white, almost silver color. He wore simple yellow fabrics with green leaf patterns and had white hair. His skin lacked pigment in most places.

RUDDY

Next to him was the fifth boy, the youngest of the group, maybe fourteen or fifteen. If the stories held true, the boy was a Feral Child living alone in the woods. Many rumors circulated about him, most of which were too bogus for the civilized to believe.

He wove his clothes from the fabrics the wild provided him. Adorned in apparel crafted from the supple hides of animals, he appeared animalistic at first glance. He crafted a unique armor, a harmonious fusion of sturdy tree bark and resilient metals he either stole or smelted himself. A helmet decorated with feathers, metals, and dry grasses rested atop his head. His cheeks also bore streaks of red paint that ran above his nostrils. The few who met him called him Ruddy because of his red hair and cheeks. Having grown up in the untamed forests, he possessed an innate ability to live in harmony with nature; his knowledge of it extended far beyond mere understanding to a deep symbiotic connection.

AKIMU

This sixth stranger proved challenging to see, as if he were a blur. Only the outline of his figure was visible, and even that barely reflected light. Haven soon concluded who it was. By all indications, it was who he thought to be only a myth: a Flame Shadow. The fire's light flickered, giving the figure some shape, but again, only glimpses were visible for fractions of a second. Haven, who studied the Flame Shadow mythology, concluded that he saw a Veiled Mangto—something, he concluded, impossible. But after sitting, this blur lowered a hood and removed his cloak. His invisibility vanished. All the others looked at him with controlled amazement. This individual was indeed a member of the Flame Shadow. Named Akimu, no other young man matched his cunning.

3

STRANGERS

The young men cast suspicious glances at each other as the fire crackled and the night's chorus of crickets filled the air. They had journeyed from distant lands, drawn by the enigma of a supposed hero, who, to their surprise, was nothing more than an ordinary adolescent. Their expectations for this leader rapidly diminished, yet a lingering curiosity kept them here.

The king studied their faces and then continued to implore them. "We are on the brink of destruction by what some call an earthquake. It seeks to destroy the island. You will unite and defeat this enemy, or we will crumble with it into the sea."

The Geezer lifted his head and added, "This is no ordinary earthquake. Ages ago, long before man occupied this land, a powerful vermian creature lifted the island from the seas. After doing so, it fell into a deep sleep. Millennia has passed, and so it awakens."

Haven's upper lip curled. He didn't believe it, not for a moment. He turned to the Geezer standing beside him. "Vermian creature?" He scoffed, dismissing the idea. "That's an old child's tale."

Upset with his response, Jehu leaned in toward Haven. "Do not dismiss this danger, lad."

"That rockworm is a fable told to scare little children," Haven muttered.

Hearing Haven's disbelief and disturbed by it, Sven wielded his axe and shield. "This is our leader? A weak dog'd rather lead me!"

Ruddy sprang up, waving his hand dismissively. "I traveled all this way for nothing? We're wasting our time."

Epoch, the Giant, whose low voice rumbled his gravelly concern, boomed out for all to feel: "He doesn't believe in the danger?"

"He will in time," the king countered. "This is the first he has heard of it. He lives south of the mountains, far from the shaking lands."

"Let me convince him," Sven sneered, pounding his fist into his hand.

While the six others muttered their doubts, Haven stared across the fire at the man he admired. "My king, why am I told this now in front of strangers who expect to find a leader?"

Drowned out by the six young men's rising complaints, Haven's question fell short. Like a father among children, King Aku took control of their gripping. "Silence, all of you!" His rotund voice moved them into silence. "Everything will be explained in time," the king said. "I will introduce you to the one who will make all things clear. Gamba Tru, tell these young men the dangers that await them."

All seven young men shuddered at hearing that name. They froze and wished it wasn't true, especially Haven. It can't be Gamba Tru.

A shadow stepped toward the fire and into the light. Lunar, whose hands shook with fright, gasped, "Gamba Tru, the savage?"

A Buccaneer emerged from the darkness, dreadlocks cascading down his shoulders. The flickering firelight revealed the intricate layers of his clothing, a black leather jacket with gold emblems, pins, and buttons. His eyes gleamed with tales of the sea, and authority emanated from the ornate trinkets hanging from his scarf and vest. The jacket had shoulder pads embroidered with yellow feathers. His gold earrings shimmered in the flame's light as he carried himself with the swagger of a killer and a true lord of maritime lore. This man was undoubtedly from the East Isles of Tortuga Nue.

Gamba Tru held his head high, noting their dread. They all knew of him as a reputed killer. Each heard the stories from the East Isles and the reports of his many murders. After all, he was the King of the Brethren of the Coast. None of them dared challenge him or his words. They knew that what he spoke was always the truth, for the words of a Buccaneer King never held deceit.

Haven stood, but Jehu pushed him back down to his seat. "King Aku would never side with an enemy of the Hadzian Kingdom," he whispered sharply to the Geezer. "A Buccaneer hasn't stepped foot in San Hadza for twenty years. He is breaking the peace treaty by just being here."

"He is here to protect peace," Jehu claimed into Haven's ear.

"But he is our enemy."

Jehu arched an eyebrow. "Not today, lad."

Gamba Tru inspected the seven young men with contempt. "Strange," he said, his voice gruff and his Spaniard accent strong. "I was told you were worthy of facing this peril, but all I see are bickering children." He turned his attention squarely on Haven. "And you, the shepherd. When you are most needed, you plead ignorance. It seems we have a coward in our midst."

Haven peered across the flames at the Buccaneer, who awaited his reply. He clenched his fists with a scowl, eager to call this man out as the Buccaneer brute he was.

"Convince me this vermian creature exists, and I will show you a leader," he said demandingly, his chest puffed out. "I am not a gullible kid convinced by mere stories."

Gamba Tru smirked, his eyes narrowing with disdain. "So be it, kid."

The Buccaneer reached into his pocket, pulled out what looked like sand, and tossed it over the fire. It combusted and sent sparks into the air. Within seconds, the stale scent attracted hundreds of fireflies.

A brilliant yellow glow illuminated the ground below, and the multitude of fireflies rang a low buzz. Jehu handed Haven a rolled-up map and asked him to unfurl it.

"The light will reveal the journey you will embark on," he said. Haven opened it, and the six others unsealed and opened theirs.

As Haven inspected the map, a route appeared under the fireflies' light, weaving upwards. "The northern hills of Hadza and the neutral occupancy," he whispered, studying the long course.

"In our youth," Gamba continued. "King Aku and I traveled this same route. We made it through the mist and reached the summit. We witnessed the creature firsthand. We are the ones spoken of in what you call a child's tale. We ascended to the peak only to be cast down."

With the seven's absolute full attention, Gamba explained their mission. "We travel north, starting tomorrow—in the Hadzian hills. I am to train you to fight the creature. Once we reach the Neutral Occupancy, we will continue north to the caves. After you pass through them, you will proceed without our guidance. This shepherd, named Haven, will lead you through the Western Bleak and up the Blind Mountains to the Breathing Summit atop the Moving Mountain."

"He isn't offering us purpose. This is suicide." Haven muttered to the Geezer, who dismissed him quickly.

The six others looked over the map's details. Some grew fearful, such as Lunar, who buried his head in his hands. The map convinced others of certain death, for what lay ahead contained untold risks and dangers. The Western Bleak was unoccupied for a reason.

King Aku, Gamba Tru, and Jehu waited for them to respond. One of the seven was quick to speak his mind.

"The Neutral Occupancy is a shelter for thieves and murderers. Why dare travel there?"

"It is the quickest route to the caves," Gamba replied.

Another spoke, "Why not ride up through the Palelands and climb the east side of the mountains? There is safe passage there."

"Not anymore," Gamba explained. "Our enemy is destroying the mountainside as we speak. It is in ruins."

King Aku stepped forward and spoke, "Hundreds of the island's strongest men have died climbing it." The king surveyed the youth, "The vermian creature sleeps with one eye open. Her root system spans across the entire island. It is capable of great destruction. Her roots seek, find, and destroy."

One of them protested, "But the Western Bleak is a wasteland. The Native's jungles sit alongside it to the west. They are hostile and eager to kill invaders. Even if we survive and reach the Blind Mountains, a man cannot see his hand before his face."

"The dense mist is poison," another alleged. "Those who breathe it choke on their vomit."

"That is not true." Gamba insisted. "The journey is difficult, but it must be traveled."

The Feral Boy, known as Ruddy, stood up and protested. "But it is impossible for us to make this journey! We are young travelers!"

Lunar added his timidity, "I am incapable of such a feat."

"I am not traveling with a Pulveran wimp!" Sven shouted, his oversized armor clanking together as he stood from his seat.

"Quiet, quiet." King Aku said, motioning for them to sit. "Have you not felt the earthquakes?"

They nodded and confirmed, "Yes."

"They have intensified, haven't they?"

They nodded again, "Yes."

He looked around at each of them. "Why do doubts consume you?" All of them remained silent. "When have two kings and a Geezer summoned you?"

Six of them replied in unison, "Never."

Haven remained silent, staring into the fire, seeking clarity. *I do not believe any of this.*

"Why us?" Haven asked the king. The others turned their heads his way. "Every kingdom has armies. Are we not mere youth? Why would two kings and a Geezer recruit seven amateurs? Aren't greater men at your disposal?"

The Buccaneer, whose fixed gaze narrowed into slits, gleamed with a fierce intensity reflecting the fire between him and Haven. He tilted his head and whispered something to Aku. The king nodded and replied, "Go on, tell them what they should know."

"Yes, you are right, shepherd boy," Gamba replied. "Why would we seek juveniles for such a task? We are desperate, that's why, and time is not our ally." He lowered his head. His voice became hoarse. "Each kingdom has sent their finest warriors to fight the creature. But many have died in their climb to the summit. We are at the end of our reserves. The last of the kingdom's soldiers embark upon her now. Most injured and weary. Some are even recreant."

"You've kept this hidden from the people," one of them remarked.

"Yes," King Aku admitted. "Ignorance is one way to keep peace. You seven are viable young men, uniquely skilled in your people's ways. But the quality we deem more important is something your inexperience provides you. Unlike our hardened, leaden soldiers, you have what they do not—the innocence of youth—the naivety to victory."

"You want us because we're gullible?" the young Norseman asked, pushing the edge of his axe down into the dirt.

"No, my boy," Jehu reacted, standing before them. "We want you because zeal and belief are not the possession of all men. We have assembled every sort of warrior, yet hopelessness remains. It was my idea to find young men to join the battle. Forty years ago, these two kings who stand before you came closest to defeating the creature, and they were young when they fought it—young, like yourselves."

The seven young men looked back at the kings and marveled at this accomplishment.

"You see," Jehu continued, "The exhausting pain that comes with defeat and age does not rest on your shoulders. You seven have not tasted the failures that come with war. You are dreamers, fresh with a new spirit. Since our enemy is ancient, we will send it youth."

"You are desperate," one of them said coldly.

Despite this, Haven found Jehu's words most inspiring. "You truly believe seven adolescents can do this?" He asked.

Jehu spoke most assuredly, "Yes, lad. In my experience, belief in victory spurs conquest. A champion's faith in his efforts incites triumph."

Gamba stepped forward. "Aku and I weren't always kings and decorated men or war. We were once young like yourselves. We almost accomplished the impossible. With our knowledge and your spirit, we can defeat the enemy. I will provide you all the materials needed to make the journey. So do not doubt. You seven can finish what we started."

Seeing all of them attentive and inspired, King Aku boldly commanded, "The time for discussion is over. Those of you who will commit your way to this quest, prepare to do so honorably."

Under the yellow light of the fireflies, Gamba Tru then proclaimed, "May the path to victory begin here, under the stars of San Hadza. This assembly of seven young strangers from the kingdoms of Wunduria will join a quest and covenant that will prevail and endure all sufferings."

And so the six strangers to San Hadza committed themselves. They did so in this order:

Epoch, son of Mammonthal, a Tribesman from the Painted Tribe. He committed his way, offering his fists and power.

Sven, son of Gorl, a Norseman from the Norse lands. He committed his way, offering his axe, shield, and bravery.

Bluff, son of Darius, a Drifter from the Anthills. He committed his way, offering his red staff and insight.

Lunar, son of Skyth, an albino Pulveran from the white trees of Pulver. He committed his way, offering his skin as a source of light.

Ruddy, son to Connor, the Feral Boy from the pocket within the Nether Forest. He committed his way, offering his slingshot and union with the wild.

And Akimu, son to the Flame Shadow. He committed his way, offering his fire blades and gifts with illusion and guile.

Under the stars of San Hadza, each committed their way to this Assemblage and its purpose.

After this, the six young men turned their attention toward Haven, who remained skeptical. He couldn't help but feel the influence of the adventure laid out before him. The call to heroism stirred something deep within him, igniting a spark of bravery he couldn't ignore. His green pendant glimmered as it rested upon his chest.

His sense of duty surged through him, eclipsing his fears and doubts. He couldn't just turn away from such a worthy endeavor. *If an evil is up in the Blind Mountains, and I do not challenge it, what type of man does that make me?*

Still across the fire, the Buccaneer leered at him with narrowed eyes of scrutiny. "Haven June," he said in his gruff, raspy voice, "a foreigner to Wunduria and shepherd to the king, rise."

With all eyes on him, including the kings, Haven trembled. He stood up, trying to hide his nervousness. So he lifted his chin and stared across the fire at the Buccaneer.

Gamba spoke slyly, "To this Assemblage, do you commit your way?"

Haven's mind ran through an endless cycle of doubts: *How can I join such an absurd cause?*

"What say you?" the Buccaneer questioned impatiently.

As Haven stood before them, his heart racing with anticipation, he gazed at the six young faces before him, wondering what they thought of him. Waves of fear washed over him. *Say something.*

"Speak!" Gamba demanded.

4

COMMIT ONESELF

Jehu nudged Haven's shoulder, pressuring him to respond. "You must excuse the boy," he said to the others. "He rehearses his words before he speaks—an odd habit for a leader, I understand."

Turning to Jehu, Haven whispered, "I don't understand why I'm supposed to be their leader. I don't know how to destroy a vermian creature."

Slapping Haven's shoulder, Jehu pressed him. "I told you before. Someone I trust said you can. You are the hero. You can tame the earthquake."

"But I'm not a hero," he growled. "Who told you that? I want a name."

"There's no time for explanations. Now get to it," Jehu urged him harshly, spitting as he spoke. He turned Haven around to face the others and pushed him forward.

Haven closed his eyes, agitated. His thoughts settled as he imagined what it would be like if he said yes.

"The boy's scared," Gamba concluded, chuckling.

Motivated by pure gut instinct, Haven took command of himself. He responded begrudgingly to the impatient Buccaneer.

"Quiet," he demanded. His heart pounded with sudden courage. He leered at the Gamba Tru, eager to prove the criminal wrong. He felt the six young pairs of eyes watching him. "I speak when I choose to, not when pressured."

The six others had their doubts and awaited a reason to trust him. Haven sensed this, so he straightened himself and squared his shoulders back. There was a sudden calmness in his demeanor.

"I was preparing my heart for such an important decision," he explained. He felt a poke at his side. Jehu handed him his shepherd's crook. A surge of strength swelled up through his chest.

"Yes, I commit my way to this Assemblage. I give you my crook with which I have fought wolves. Through every season, through every hardship, I have protected my sheep. They are always safe in my keep. So I give you my protection, I give you my heart, and I give you my leadership, for I am Haven, the shepherd."

His words intrigued all of them, including Gamba Tru. King Aku smiled proudly.

"I am the one who will guide you safely through danger because failure has no hold on me," Haven continued. "I am not afraid of what lies ahead of us; because of this, I will earn your trust."

This impressive commitment assured the six others. They saw him as someone with authority. Each of them willed their hearts to follow him.

Sven pounded his axe into the ground excitedly. Epoch pounded his chest. Ruddy tilted his head, fascinated by his new leader's conviction.

"Then it is so," Gamba slowly announced.

Bluff walked over to Haven, staring sternly into him. "I will follow you," he said.

Sven then walked over to him. "I, too, will follow you."

And one after another, the young men all spoke in kind. "I will follow you."

Jehu smiled, commending Haven for his improvisational skills. "You're a natural. I just knew it," he concluded before exiting to find sleep. The Buccaneer, however, was still suspicious. He kept his gaze across the fire at Haven.

"Get your sleep, boy. We set out at dawn," he said to him curtly.

A rush of regret lingered as Haven returned to his tree home. *What have I gotten myself into?*

~~~

King Aku took Gamba Tru to a quiet spot near his arboretum. After lighting a lantern, the King sensed Gamba's frustration. "What concerns you?"

"This whole endeavor." Gamba hesitated, struggling to explain himself. "What are we doing here, Mikel?" he groaned, calling the king by his first name. "Assembling youth because they believe in victory?" He covered his eyes with his hand and rubbed between them. He traveled a long way to get there. His tiredness showed. "Jehu assembled a fool's hope. I'm a fool for considering it. I should be out there climbing the peaks, daring to slay the monster myself. I should be there now, getting my revenge."

Mikel Aku sighed; his once solid stature, now stooped with age, sat with a meager spirit. "Your heart is still young. I wish I could say the same, but I've grown weary." His voice carried the weight of many years gone by, mixed with resignation. "Old injuries are showing themselves. The Faction Wars may be years behind us, but my body remembers all too well. My flesh and spirit are weak."

Gamba's respectful tone reflected his empathy for his friend's aging. "Time passes quickly. Injuries do not."

"Time is not on our side. If only we could shuttle them through the mountains by air."

"I tried to attain a vessel. I even dared to commandeer one." Gamba admitted. "But I do not have the influence I once had with the galleon commander. In his eyes, I am no longer the king of the East Isles; I'm exiled on behalf of the new rising powers. Only the brethren defend me now, as does my sister. It's up to her to lead the armada to the summit."

Mikel knew none of this. He sunk his head low to his chest. "This is unfortunate for you. My condolences, Gamba." Mikel smiled weakly. "But your sister is reliable. Glori is as honorable as you and quick with a sword."

Trapped in concern, Gamba stared blankly into the darkness of night. "The Council and our spies stand behind these six young ones. This I know. But I wonder about the seventh one, this shepherd of yours. Why him? Why travel this far for one boy?"

"He is remarkable," Mikel replied. "I certainly vouch for him. Test him out, and you will see."

"So he is your recommendation?"

Mikel pouted. "No. This morning, a council emissary informed me of Haven's procurement. Jehu confirmed it with his arrival. I find it odd to receive the news so late. This has unfolded unexpectedly."

"So the council recommended him?"

Mikel shook his head. "A secret one demands his presence. One who knows the potential he possesses."

"A secret one?" Gamba asked, furrowing his brow.

"A wise foreigner," he replied, rubbing his stiff neck. "Jehu's been most discreet about the matter."

Gamba's face wrinkled further. "A foreigner to Wunduria? Strange that we depend on a secret one's word during a most desperate time."

"It is desperation that has led us here. I understand your skepticism, and I, too, have some. We dare assemble a team with such inexperience. They're not warriors, not men of fame, but mere youth."

"They're fools," Gamba replied.

"Maybe. But so were we at that age when we fought the creature."

"That's what scares me, Mikel. We failed to destroy it." Gamba placed his hand on the hilt of his sword, a habit his warrior heart never abandoned, always ready for battle. "Can Haven leave behind this place of peace and comfort?"

"You must make him," Mikel replied. "Teach him all you know."

"In such a short time? That won't happen." Gamba paced, searching his doubts. "What makes him capable of destroying the creature? What does he have that the rest of us don't?"

Mikel Aku rose to his feet, puzzled, like Gamba. "That is what you must find out."

~~~

Birds welcomed the sunrise with their usual chirping. A cool morning breeze entered a window, grazing Haven's skin as he lay in bed. For an instance of time, he thought the morning to be as typical as any. He even rolled over to peer out his window. He smiled to see that early hue of a new morning awakening in dawn's darkness—a color he found inspiring. But like a shock to his body, the memory of the previous night jolted him up from his bed. *The Geezer, the Buccaneer, the Assemblage!*

The urgency of the situation propelled him into action. He hurried to his storage trunk. From it, he retrieved his backpack and a sling bag. With fitful motions, he quickly packed each with the items he deemed essential for his trip. He threw in clothes, food, and tools. "Can't forget my boots," he muttered, reminding himself of the harsh realities that awaited him.

"Everything? Do I have everything?" he asked himself, looking around his small home. He felt for his necklace. He sighed, feeling it hang from his chest. "Phew."

He shut the door to his tree home, his heart heavy with the weight of his decision to join this quest. He questioned whether he was making the right choice. He closed his eyes and exhaled to calm his thoughts.

"Morning, my friend." King Aku's warm and familiar voice cut through the excitement. He joined Haven there with a comforting presence and two cups of coffee. "Mornings are dreary without Kawha, aren't they?" he remarked, a hint of a smile on his lips.

Haven bowed his head and replied, exasperated, "Thank you." He accepted the cup happily and sipped it. "This is just what I needed."

The king chuckled and sipped from his cup. "Let us enjoy the morning. We'll walk toward the rising sun and watch dawn have its way on creation."

After setting his bags down, Haven joined him. They took a stroll, walking silently. They listened to the dawn chorus and reflected on the beauty. The stroll led them to a bench near the estate gardens. Off in the distance were the horses belonging to the party of young men who slept inside a wagon. Near a fire, Gamba Tru and Jehu sat eating breakfast.

Noticing them, the king turned to Haven. "Why did you believe those two men?" he asked. Interested in his response, almost eager to know it, Aku leaned in toward him. "They are strangers to you, so please tell me."

"I'm not sure," he replied, seeing the concern in the king's eyes. "I listened to them because of you."

"Because of me?" he asked in an ambivalent tone. "Or is it because you want it to be true?"

"What makes you say that?" Haven asked, thinking the king was on to something.

"I've watched you grow up here on my land," he said with a kind smile. "I've watched you grow from a daring and courageous boy to a sensible young man," the king recalled in a comforting tone. "When you and your mother made this place your home, I often heard your desires to be a hero one day."

"I forgot about that," Haven said, grinning.

The king looked out at the green fields that surrounded them. "It seemed all boyish talk, but I saw your potential. If it were a hero you wanted to be, I would allow you to train as one without the commitment, without transparency, so your mother wouldn't worry."

"What do you mean?" Haven asked.

"I made you a shepherd," he chuckled. "A hero protects innocence. Sheep are vulnerable. They require care and attention."

Haven snickered. "Yes, I remember how difficult it was—trying to make them return to their pen. They resisted me. I hated it."

"But you didn't hate them," he said, nudging Haven's arm. "A hero does not hate the innocent or the weak. He strengthens them. When they required more, you adjusted your methods. You became gentle, you became patient. Instead of pushing them, you led them. Now, when you go out ahead, they follow you because you are their shepherd," the king said assuredly.

Haven placed his hand over his chest, pleased by his years of shepherding.

"In your heart, you're still that boy who wants to be a hero, protecting peace," the king said, poking Haven's shoulder. "That is why you listened to those men."

Haven finally admitted out loud, "I want to be a hero. I want it to be my purpose in life."

"Those men offer you the chance to become one, not for sheep, but for people."

Haven reflected on the opportunity. "How do I go from being a shepherd to a leader of men?"

"You'll figure that out along the way," Aku winked.

Sitting back against the bench's backrest, Haven shrugged. "In moments like this, I wish my father were here. He would teach me like you do."

The king put his arm around his shoulder. "Remember, a father instructs with discipline because it is what his child needs. I have been many things to you, but I am not your father."

Haven nodded. "I know, my king. And I thank you for being a strong influence on me. I needed it. I just wonder why I have this instinct inside me. I long to help others. I desire to be a hero. Maybe my father would explain to me why."

"Maybe. But fathers do not raise heroes; they raise sons," he replied, patting Haven on the shoulder. "Your trip will be long and challenging. With your mother away in Zyra, she'll know nothing of it. Her heart can desire the things paradise offers instead of worrying for you."

Haven chuckled. "I'm assuming the queen didn't mind leaving troubles behind?"

"It was her idea," the king admitted amusingly. "Men need to protect peace while women and children enjoy the safety and comforts they deserve."

"Why is that true, my king?"

He replied with a stern look. "The future is planted in them. A man must protect it, even if it breaks him."

"While we are broken, they are made strong," Haven summarized. The king nodded.

Haven stood, ready to fetch his things. "I hope to be victorious."

"You will be. But be on guard; You must abandon your youthful ways to survive the journey to the summit. Peace and comfort will not get you there. Maturity comes at a cost—it always does."

5
LEAVING FOR ADVENTURE

The Assemblage made their way down the dirt road leading out of San Hadza's capital, Ekurh. The seven were in awe of the city's grandeur. Ekurh was a place where dignified dwellers and riches abounded. The brick roads, marble carvings, and intricate stone buildings revealed the city's prosperity. Trees and vegetation abounded.

"Far too elegant for me," the short Norseman, Sven, remarked, even though he blushed when seeing the young Hadzian girls smiling his way while singing.

As they made their way through a market, the seven noticed the curious faces of the inhabitants who lined the streets. The people of San Hadza were not used to seeing such a diverse group of travelers. Epoch, the Giant Tribesman who lumbered along with them, only added to the bewilderment of the onlookers.

He complained about the people's constant staring. His height was worthy of gawking, though he did not like it. It was difficult for the people not to question what a Geezer, a Giant, an albino Pulveran, a freckled Feral Boy, a circlet-wearing Drifter, and a short Vig Norseman were doing in their city. Not that the dwellers of Ekurh minded such things. The Assemblage added excitement to the people's day and gave much reason to converse and speculate.

Haven couldn't help but revel in the attention their motley crew attracted. The unusual excitement in the air was infectious, and he walked with a spring in his step. By the time they left the city, their group had become a topic of discussion. Their departure left the city abuzz with speculation. Akimu, as always, remained veiled and unseen, an expert in the Flame Shadow way.

Despite leaving the excitement of the city behind them, the Assemblage continued their journey with a sense of purpose. They had a mission, and nothing would stand in their way.

To keep the people of Ekurh from fear, Gamba Tru met the Assemblage well outside the city. From there, he led them through the Hadza Plains and Hills, riding his black horse at the front of their caravan. Jehu coached the wagon behind him and joined the young men's horses together to pull it. "It'll lessen their burden," he claimed.

Haven requested he ride his stallion, Thunder, separately. Sven refused to join his horse with the others, stubbornly and arrogantly keeping his chin up and lingering in the back behind the wagon. He kept his shield and axe in their rightful places. "An unarmed Norseman is a stupid Norseman," he claimed.

Though the quest presented the young men with trepidation, they all handled it bravely. Epoch, Bluff, Lunar, and Ruddy sat inside the wagon's covered wooden bed. They played games—dice mostly—and joked, as adolescents do. Epoch's giant presence and mild temper gave them a sense of safety, while Lunar fretted over anything discomforting. Mostly, Bluff remained his stoic self, expressionless and mouth shut.

Ruddy reclined, finding the company pleasant to be with. This entire affair was more than out of the ordinary for him. Most of his life he spent alone in the wild among the land and creation. But he adjusted well, watching each of his comrades with a grin. He even removed his helmet to reveal his greasy red hair. Lunar quickly told him he smelled awful as he pulled up a section of the wagon's cover to allow some fresh air. "When was the last time you bathed?" he asked.

Ruddy thought for a moment, scratching his head. "Oh, some time ago in the streams of Thyme."

Lunar plugged his nose and moved to the other side of the wagon. "Well, you stink. I have soap you can use and some lavender to rub on ya."

"Thanks?" Ruddy said with a puzzled expression.

The glorious terrain was a vast expanse of lush greenery, stretching as far as the eye could see, all under blue skies and white puffy clouds.

Deer, horses, and yak occupied the rolling hills. Goats and groundhogs fed on the flat plains. It was a wild and accessible place, with grass swaying in the sunlight. The fresh streams gave the Assemblage and their horses ample opportunity to quench their thirst. It also gave Ruddy time to bathe and wash his messy hair. Lunar suggested that he keep the soap.

Occasionally, they passed tiny farmhouses owned by simple people. The farther they traveled through the plains, the fewer houses they passed. A farmer here or there and tiny homes built from stones sat in comfortable surroundings. The enchanting peace filled all their hearts, even Gamba's.

Akimu traveled with them, but secretly. Jehu assured Haven that the Flame Shadow wouldn't always remain unseen. "Akimu's entire existence is a secret," the Geezer explained. "But I trust he will rid his discretion. Just don't forget he's there because he is."

Haven tried to converse with Gamba, who quickly advised him to get to know the others first. So Haven did just that. He joined Sven, the Norseman, behind the wagon.

Upon his trusty steed, Sven rode with a steadfast sense of duty. His horned helmet perched precariously atop his head, its size mismatched to his small stature, causing it to wobble with each rhythmic stride of his horse. Despite the comical sight of the oversized headpiece, there was a weight of responsibility in Sven's demeanor as he rode forth, his eyes fixed on the path ahead and his heart filled with the call of honor.

His brutal view of life fit the cliche of a Vig Norseman. He boasted about those he knew back home, especially his older brothers and his father, who were fighters and drinkers. He spoke as if he were certain about everything he said.

"I have long hair because only those considered fit for battle shave their heads," he told Haven. "I am not yet a Drang, which is a great shame to myself. My father took my brothers up to the summit without me. They left me behind with the children," he further explained, disgraced by it. "When we return from slaying the vermian beast, I will have proven my worth. Then I will be a mighty warrior. I will earn my place among the men of fame."

Their travels through the land continued to be rewarding. Along the road were Bubble Plants. The floating nectar bubbles were plenty, which kept the bees and hummingbirds busy. Wild Gigant Horses joined the seven and the two mentors at a water hole, which pleasantly surprised them all. The majestic, giant creatures were indeed impressive. They were twice the size of an average horse. Even Thunder found it challenging to blend in with them without giving way to fear.

Blue Whisper Butterflies were not so scared. They rested on the heads of these giant horses, maybe to relax or say hello—the gentlest of things on top of powerful juggernauts. Gamba told the seven to appreciate the moment's beauty and consider what was at stake. "This peace and beauty is irreplaceable. We save it, or we lose it."

Each of the seven expressed out loud their thoughts. "I stay nowhere for long, and I've never stuck by anyone's side. Many have called me a scoundrel, things like that. But even I know our quest is good and right," Bluff said, standing tall.

All agreed with a nod. It was the first time all seven shared expressions from the heart. Eventually, they laughed together, finding common ground on many things.

It allowed Haven a chance to speak with Bluff, the one he found most interesting. Most considered him a mere Drifter, giving his loyalty to no kingdom. His brown freckled skin glistened in the sunlight. With a red staff gripped firmly, he exuded a distinct dauntlessness borne from the deserts of the Anthills.

To Bluff's delight, he and Haven connected quickly, agreeing on many things. Their personalities were conducive to getting along. They both shared similar ideals, even if each hadn't known it yet. There was an energy between them, like kin.

As evening approached, the group traveled at a much quicker pace. With every grassy hill ventured, the bonds of comradeship grew stronger. Jehu sang old hymns that none of them knew. The Geezer's voice was enjoyable to hear, so none complained. Before setting up camp for the night, they passed the Queen Eshe statue beside the silver stone road. She was a queen from ages ago who fought off a giant bear that killed her husband. The bear came to be known as King Killer. The statue was a memorial built where she fought the enormous beast. Sven and Epoch found it most interesting. Lunar joked that the fabled bear was still alive, roaming the darker parts of forests.

Sven rolled his eyes. "It's no fable," he alleged. "The creature is still out there. I will be the one to kill it one day."

Finally, they rested inside their tents. They had traveled a long way since the morning. Gamba gave strict orders to sleep. It was a command easy to obey, as they gladly yielded and did just so. Haven's last thoughts before he slept were of consequences this quest would bring, such as if he'd ever see his mother again. And if trusting this Gamba Tru would prove disastrous. *This seemed far too enjoyable of a day to be considered training. What does he have prepared for us tomorrow?*

6

WAKE UP

In the darkest of night, Gamba woke the seven using a large cymbal. The jarring metallic timbre rang over their tents, instantly waking all seven. They awoke frightened, and each panicked as he rang it several times. Gamba shouted out for all to hear, "Find your weapons! Quick!"

Epoch, who slept inside the wagon, jerked so aggressively that he tipped it over to its side. The unhitched horses squealed and fled into the darkness of night.

The other six stood up, bewildered. They stumbled many times, looking for their weapons. In the darkness, they panicked, utterly unprepared to defend themselves.

Haven was the first to exit his tent. He held his shepherd's crook out before him, swinging at nothing. In front of him, he noticed the campfire, or at least where the fire once was. Only the dying embers remained. He spun around in search of an enemy. "What is happening?" he shouted.

Lunar exited his tent in desperation, retreating into the field. His glowing skin gave away his nudeness. It was customary for a Pulveran to sleep this way. "Help me!" he cried in his retreat.

"I'm awake!" Sven shouted, emerging from his tent. He held his axe and shield, ready for combat. "Have no fear!" he called with clueless bravado. He swung his shield, hitting someone in the head.

"Ouch!" Bluff responded, falling backward.

"Ah ha! Take that!" Sven howled.

Akimu joined Haven near the embers. He stood in martial arts pose, shouting a typical Flame Shadow battle cry: "KIAI!"

Ruddy rolled out from his tent with his helmet on backward. "I can't see!" he shouted. He nervously pulled his slingshot out and fired a shot that, by chance, hit Epoch, who was busy punching air (what Ruddy didn't know was that rather than firing a pellet, he shot a strawberry instead. He kept some in his pocket as a snack). It hit Epoch directly in the face.

Finally, a high-pitched whistle caught their attention. It was Gamba who poured rum over the embers, igniting a fire. The burst of flames revealed the cause of all this fear and commotion. They saw it to be their mentor and menacing agitator. Behind the fire, Gamba Tru stood scowling. Of course, Jehu found it all humorous, but he kept his laughter to himself (mostly).

"Pathetic, all of you!" Gamba shouted. "Take your positions around the fire, now!" On command, the six of them collected, trying to compose themselves. They looked at one another, exasperated and ashamed.

"Where's the glowing kid?" Gamba asked angrily. They all looked around for Lunar. Some of them spotted him still retreating far off into the distance. His sprint was fantastic. "One of you go get him," Gamba demanded. Haven ran off toward the Pulveran, dismayed.

Upon return, Lunar draped a blanket over his nakedness, too embarrassed to make eye contact with the others. Now fully intact, the seven lowered their heads as the Buccaneer berated them. One by one, he harassed them. He said their poor reaction to the unexpected was never to happen again.

"You will die at the hands of your stupidity!" he yelled. "Your actions tonight leave me no choice but to break you. You will need the harshest training to reach the summit." They felt the detest in his words. A great torment filled their hearts as they felt guilty of much folly. Even Akimu, an expert in sure-minded calmness, shook with uncertainty. They had the same question racing through their minds: *What did I get myself into?*

"You are mine to destroy and mine to rebuild," Gamba warned. "I will break you, and then I will fix you!"

~ ~ ~

Far before sunrise, the seven underwent rigorous drills and exercises, testing the physical skills Gamba knew they would need. Quick to correct and always harsh, he disciplined them with force. "This means your life!" He yelled. "What good are you dead?"

In the shadow of rugged cliffs, this band of young men trained under the tutelage of the seasoned Buccaneer. Under his watchful eye, they learned the art of swashbuckling, a style of combat that demanded finesse and flair. It is a daring and romantic form of dueling fueled with passion and a lust for greatness.

For years, Gamba trained boys into capable men. He knew how to infiltrate a boy's mind and heart and reach their conscience. As for these seven, he found each boy's physical, emotional, and mental weaknesses.

Lunar was the first to give up when he saw the others succeed. "You will learn to live in the shadow and survive it," Gamba told him.

Epoch hated any task that didn't involve using his strength. While others deftly navigated through puzzles of strategy and cunning, he struggled to find his footing in the labyrinth of intellect and style. Accustomed to relying on his brawn to conquer adversity, he pounded his fists and screamed, casting doubt upon his boundless spirit. "A blaze of trickery will become your secret weapon."

Akimu refused to speak, finding it difficult to communicate with the others. Ruddy wouldn't accept a helping hand. Sven embraced the competition but gave into self-doubt when his small size stymied him. The drifter, Bluff, reacted begrudgingly to leadership, so Gamba tested his ability to listen and obey.

The morning felt long, and the afternoon didn't bring relief. The sun beat down upon their faces and bodies. Gamba allowed them zero food, zero water, and no time to catch their breath. Instead, far into a forest, he placed sustenance atop a cliff. He taught them the fundamentals of climbing. Then, he explained the task. "Run through the forest. Find the rock wall and climb it. Three portions of food and water await those who make it. They belong to the first three. The others will go hungry."

The seven darted into the forest, sprinting to the rock mass. Akimu and Haven reached the top first. Lunar reached the top shortly after they did. Sven was next but cursed in failure upon seeing the others already there. But for the three victors, they discerned what necessity demanded. They encouraged the others to finish the climb.

After reaching the top, all seven shared the food and water. Gamba applauded their efforts and offered advice: "To survive the dangers ahead of you and ascend to the summit, you must give more than you take. Without sustaining your brothers, you, too, will fail. You achieve victory collectively."

They continued the day's training deep into the evening. As the shades of dusk fell upon them, they crossed an extended length of grassland. Once across, they settled in a grove filled with fig trees. The seven washed up in a stream, each exhausted, with cuts and bruises. While Jehu helped them prepare supper, Gamba took Haven into a secluded dark forest called Trialum.

There, they dueled with swords. Gamba felt it necessary to see how his young student would perform under constant pressure. "Attack, then defend. Attack, then defend," he commanded.

Haven hated that a Buccaneer, a man who lived violently and embraced war, was his mentor. *I am not interested in this Spaniard's fierce teachings. I will defeat him.*

Gamba fought him ferociously, asking questions and demanding answers to distract the boy. "Your name is uncommon." Gamba sneered, deflecting a hit. "Who gave it to you?" He then attacked with a sequence of beats. Haven defended them off incredibly well, considering the Buccaneer's experience with a sword.

"My father did," Haven answered.

"For what purpose?" Gamba asked. "Are you to be a refuge?"

Haven defended a quick slash and dodged another. "That was his hope," he answered, staring at Gamba contemptuously.

Gamba lunged, with the point of his blade aimed at his student's chest, but Haven dodged the attempt rather well. "Your father wanted you to fight for peace?"

Haven shook his head. "Not everything is about fighting." He scoffed. "I provide peace to living things."

With many strikes, Gamba forced Haven backward. "What if the only path to peace is battle?"

Frustrated by his mentor's reasoning, he swung his blade angrily. Gamba easily parried the swing. Haven sneered at him with a question of his own. "Don't you think a man should embrace peace rather than violence?"

Gamba chuckled. "I do, but you did not answer the question."

With strength and finesse, Gamba moved with the agility of a panther stalking its prey. Though much older than Haven, he fought like a young man. "A man should know enough about peace to protect it. That is my answer." Haven replied.

"But how does he protect it?" Gamba asked, advancing upon him.

Haven defended a slash and backed off. "I don't know!"

"Answer the question! You fought wolves, did you not?" Gamba recalled swinging his blade aggressively.

"Yes, I did. To protect my sheep!" he exclaimed, deflecting another slash. Gamba moved sideways with ease, listening to his protégé speak.

"But I had to fight them. Each time, every time! They would not scare away," he said, pivoting and lunging forward. Gamba diverted the attack. They circled one another, both ready to attack—proof that Haven wanted to achieve greatness.

"So you had to fight to protect the peace your sheep enjoyed?" Gamba prodded, circling closer to him.

"Yes, your point?" Haven recoiled, his jaw tense.

Gamba swung a daring strike. Haven ducked just in time and kicked Gamba's foot. It was a fine hit and just enough to move Gamba back, who found the strike amusing. Haven caught his breath as he stood, rattled and anxious.

"What is a man to you?" Gamba asked. But Haven did not reply. He hadn't an answer to give. "Should a man be dangerous?" Gamba then asked.

Searching for an answer and his next move, Haven replied with what he always believed to be true, "No. A man should be peaceful."

"Peaceful? But you proved dangerous to the wolf," Gamba reasoned. He then advanced and struck Haven's sword. Haven backed off, frustrated, clenching his sword tighter, but Gamba did not allow him his moment of rest. "So, answer me. What is a man to you?"

Haven stammered but could not answer. "He is..."

"Is he a terror?" Gamba asked, cutting Haven's hand with the point of his blade, an intentional scratch used for distraction. Haven drew back, covering his hand, but he had little time to recover. Gamba's blade was too quick.

Haven backed into a tree. Gamba swung again. Haven defended the hit, but at a cost. Gamba pushed his blade against Haven's. The Buccaneer proved too strong. Haven spit in his face. Gamba laughed. "I do not fear your saliva."

He pushed his blade further against Haven's, pressing their blades against Haven's chest. Haven clenched his jaw, feeling the blade push against his clothing. He used his foot to push Gamba away from him. It was just enough to escape.

He quickly retreated, but Gamba pursued, towering over him. His frightful appearance darkened in the shadows of the dark forest. Gamba swung at him again and again.

"You're a monster!" Haven shouted, dodging the swings.

"A man must be!" he responded, pursuing him.

Haven knew not how to reply. He feared the Buccaneer. "You're cruel!" He shouted back. "You're a nightmare!" He swung desperately. Gamba thrust forward; his sword enveloped Havens at the handle. He circled the hilt and disarmed him. Haven's sword flung into the air and out of reach. He stumbled and fell to the ground. With his face in the dirt, he rolled over to find the point of Gamba's sword at his neck.

A smirking Gamba spoke quietly. "Nightmares are inevitable. But are you prepared for them?"

Haven gasped for air. He closed his eyes, disappointed by the defeat. Gamba returned his sword to his sheath. He then reached his hand out and helped Haven up from the ground. "You fought well, shepherd boy."

They headed to camp casually, discussing what being a man meant to both of them. Haven's idea was peace and gentleness with life.

"You speak of many good things," the grizzled Buccaneer told him. "Peace is always the final goal. When we embrace peace, it improves our lives and the lives of those around us."

Cracking his neck from side to side, Haven questioned his mentor. "So why do you speak of fighting and terror? Must a man be this way?"

"He should be capable of those things, yes," he replied. "Haven, a man should be many things. Peaceful and gentle, yes, but also willing to protect those he loves. A true man has power over his terror, using it as a tool he can wield."

"And that leads to peace?" Haven asked with a disrespectful tone. "Seems unnecessarily barbaric to me."

"Says the boy who's lived a peaceful land that he did not earn for himself," Gamba remarked.

Insulted, Haven lashed out. "Says a Pirate whose reputation is violence."

Gamba snickered. "Oh, piracy is not in my heart. There is much about the Buccaneers you do not understand."

Haven rolled his eyes. "Well, there's much about me you do not understand."

"And yet, I am trying to," Gamba added kindly. "So please, tell me what I do not know."

Humbled, reminded by his need for improvement, Haven lowered his head, "Yes, sorry. I need to remind myself you're here to teach me."

"You are still hesitant to respect me," Gamba added. "I can sense it easily."

Haven nodded and spoke honestly, "I still don't see how becoming a terror will help me become a better man."

"You're a shepherd," Gamba acknowledged. "You care for your sheep and watch over them. This takes qualities that a good man and leader should know. Gentleness, patience, you're trustworthy and watchful."

Haven nodded, pleased to hear such things.

"But you also killed a wolf?" Gamba countered.

"Yes, I had to," he replied. "It was hunting my sheep."

Gamba put his hand on Haven's shoulder. "Because you are a shepherd who protects peace. But to that wolf, you were its killer. You were a terror, but your sheep live peacefully because of it. They are still alive because you fought what sought to harm them. I consider that heroic."

Rubbing his chin, Haven replied, "To be their hero, I had to become a monster in the eyes of the enemy."

"You're beginning to understand."

Deep in thought, Haven followed Gamba to the end of the dark Trialum forest. As Gamba continued out of the forest into the soft light of dusk, he turned to find Haven standing still in thought.

"I think that's enough darkness for one day," Gamba suggested.

Haven looked up at him. "You've given me something I needed: perspective. Thank you."

Pleased with the boy, Gamba responded jokingly, "Don't thank me yet. Tomorrow might change your mind." Haven smiled and joined his mentor in what little light remained.

"Oh, one more question," Gamba added.

Haven turned to him. "Yes?"

"Did you enjoy killing the wolf?"

Haven shook his head. "No, not at all. I hated it."

Gamba nodded with a grin. "Good. When a man enjoys killing, his heart is truly lost."

7
QUESTIONS

Haven joined his comrades at a campfire, eating food and making jokes. They poked fun at one another, all in good fun. Gamba sat far away near his horse and smiled occasionally, hearing their camaraderie. They laughed and carried on about who would become the greater warrior. Of course, Sven had the most to say about the matter. Pacing back and forth in front of them all, he swore one day he'd be like his hero, the mighty Jarl of the Viking army.

"Gunnar, the greatest warrior in all the lands," he said. "Stronger than this vermian beast we pursue. You'll see."

Lunar's belly ached from the rabbit stew Jehu fed them, so he walked a reasonable distance away to relieve himself. Unfortunately for him, they saw him wherever he went. His glowing skin gave him no privacy. The others laughed, calling his bum a beacon. They saw him everywhere he hid, even when hiding behind trees.

"We can still see you!" Sven laughed.

"Stop mooning us, boy!" Bluff shouted.

"Does your wiz glow, too?" Sven added, rolling to the ground, laughing.

"Will your droppings be a night light?" Ruddy added, joining in the fun. Lunar was shy about the whole matter and cursed himself repeatedly. Haven suggested they held back their wisecracks because he was a Pulveran.

"Ah, those wimps could use some bullying," Sven remarked, quite upset he couldn't bully the boy any longer. "How will he fight our enemy if he can't take some teasing?"

After the heckling, the night's mood changed when Gamba urged them to unwind and get ready for sleep. The stars above gave the seven cause for reflection, so the conversation became serious. Their questions revealed their concerns.

"Jehu, tell us more about the vermian creature," Ruddy requested. But the old man was asleep. He had drifted off some time ago. They called for him. He moved his head ever so slightly.

"Jehu!" they shouted in unison.

He lifted his head, unbothered. "Oh, oh yes," he grumbled. "I'm awake. rockworm, you say?" He rubbed his eyes. "What would you like to know?"

"How old is the thing?" Ruddy asked, who placed his bare feet closer to the fire for warmth. Dirty things they were, with long nails.

"No one knows. Tens of thousands of years, I suppose," Jehu mumbled, still rubbing his eyes.

"But you're a Geezer." Sven asserted. "You have access to the ancient scrolls."

"Yes, I do, I do. However, the ancient scrolls are ambiguous about the vermian creature's age. They do, however, identify her with a name: Snarlag."

Lunar shivered, moving closer to the fire. "Snarlag? Sounds scary."

Sven fixated on the flames, staring intensely into them. "I wonder how it's still alive?"

"That is the conundrum," Jehu agreed. "We may never know. Truths become unreliable through the great passage of time."

Haven turned to him. "What do you mean?"

"Well, truth becomes legend, legend becomes myth, myth becomes fantasy. History is sometimes a riddle."

"Who discovered this Snarlag was still alive?" Bluff asked.

Jehu looked to Gamba. "I'll let your mentor answer this one."

Gamba walked over to them and sat down, smoking some herb. The smell was strong. Upon smelling it, Lunar sat farther away, covering his belly again, which moved Sven to roll his eyes.

"Forty years ago, in my youth, a great earthquake shook the land," Gamba said. "Leaving enough devastation to cause my father, myself, King Aku, and three others to search for answers. In our travels, we found the land in the west cracked. We followed it to the mountains, and there it disappeared into the mist. So we scaled them and reached the summit. We saw what looked like giant snakes slithering out of the ground. They were appendages from a creature breathing deep inside a hollow chamber." He said, taking a puff of his herb.

The chill in the air was bone-deep as a gust of frigid breeze swept through the camp, sending shivers down everyone's spine. The fire crackled and danced. Some moved closer to it. Amidst the unease of Gamba's retelling of his experience, a creeping sense of worry seeped into the seven. A few of them shuddered, prompting them to question if they had what it took to face the creature. Mystery lurked in Gamba's words.

"My father and I descended upon it," he continued. "The air was hot, difficult to breathe. We realized we were inside the creature's den. There it slept, in hibernation. Covered in a mess of its fleshly roots."

Epoch straightened his back. "How big was it?"

"Larger than any creature I've ever seen," Gamba answered.

Jehu lit his pipe and added what he thought to be substantial information. "The ancient scrolls tell us that the longer a rockworm lives, the further its appendages grow under the ground.

If my estimations are accurate, the worm's roots branch under all of Wunduria, growing like dendrite."

"So that's why you believe it will destroy the island?" Haven asked. Jehu gestured a confirmation.

"Are we sure this thing is a worm?" Bluff said. "Arms that slither don't sound like a worm to me."

Sven stood, eager to hear of the fight. "Gamba, you and King Aku fought it, didn't you?" His voice crackled like a child in puberty.

Gamba nodded. "Yes. Trapped and outnumbered, we fought Snarlag's roots, but there were too many. She crumbled the surroundings." Gamba's voice softened.

"But you survived," Lunar said, looking intently at Gamba's face. The seven saw vulnerability in the Buccaneer's face for the first time. There was pain behind his eyes.

"Yes, but at a cost. It grabbed hold of my father. I held on to him, but I was too weak. She pulled him into the abyss," he said, lifting his head and peering into Haven's eyes. "I can still hear her consume him. I am cursed with the memory of it."

Gamba took a final puff of his herb and tossed it into the fire. The young men waited for what he would say next. "It's been a long day. Get your rest." He recoiled and left them.

"How did he and King Aku make it out alive?" Ruddy wondered. "Are we going to hear that story?"

"Not all things are to be told, young one," Jehu said. "It is Gamba's decision what he teaches you."

"So we're all going to die," Lunar muttered.

Epoch walked past him and patted his back. "Don't lose hope, scared boy."

"I'm not scared," Lunar replied. "I'm realistic. There's a difference."

QUESTIONS

"Not when you say it," Sven said, punching Lunar's shoulder as he walked past him.

Soon, they all departed from the fire toward their tents, including Jehu. Only Haven remained peering into the flame, unsettled by his mentor's tale.

Bluff noticed Haven still sitting before the fire. "Get some sleep, Haven," he suggested. Haven did not reply. He remained there, keeping his attention on the flames.

I'll sleep when I'm tired.

~ ~ ~

The seven cooked eggs and vegetables. They sipped coffees and teas, awaiting direction from Gamba. And they soon did. He greeted them with a smile and was quite cheerful. They remembered his recoil the night before and wondered what had changed.

Their protégé appeared more than ready for the day. In the sunlight, they studied his appearance. Upon his brow, strands of silver mingled with the dark locks of his hair, evidence of the wisdom earned through years of trial and triumph. His attire befit his maritime legacy. He wore a coat of faded leather adorned with trinkets and trophies from battles won and lost. Across his puffed blouse lay a bandolier laden with pouches of powder and shot.

"Who's this guy?" Lunar jeered quietly.

Sven was just as confounded. "And what did he do with Gamba Tru?"

He looked at them with a sneaking grin. "Today, the pains of your training will increase," Gamba announced with an impish grin.

During their training, he took them to many places. They visited a cave where they found a Den of Snakes. Gamba challenged them to pass over it: "If you cannot dodge leaping snakes, you will not survive Snarlag's slithering roots."

After this, they marched to a clear lake filled with giant fish. There, they were each bitten by Fish of Fangs. Their bites were not fatal but provided a sense of pain that challenged even Epoch's tolerance. "You must tolerate the pain that comes with survival. Do not let it stop you," Gamba advised, watching the seven struggle to out-swim the nasty fish.

He next led the Assemblage of young men to a sandy hill called the Path of Resistance. With a commanding voice, he challenged them to race to the top. Little did they know, the sandy terrain contained an itchy substance that, upon contact with the skin, caused a burning sensation. As they sprinted up the hill, their bare feet sunk into a deceptive ground, and cries of surprise and pain filled the air. It was a lesson learned the hard way, a test of resilience. The Buccaneer watched closely, knowing true warriors were forged through trials and setbacks. "Never expect new places to be safe and forgiving. Not everything is as it appears."

Each walked away with rashes and burns that soon faded as they cleaned themselves at a riverbed named Riverweed. Jehu assured them it was a clean and safe place to rinse off.

After they returned to join Jehu along the roadside, Gamba Tru started them with personalized teachings. They fought with dull swords (which bothered Sven) and then with their fists (which bothered Lunar). Haven faced off against Gamba himself. Bruises, cuts, and pain were the game. Nothing so severe they couldn't prevail through, but enough to toughen them up.

Gamba explained to the seven that Snarlag's skin was as hard as the mountain it lived inside. "One cannot penetrate the skin with a mere sword. Other more sophisticated techniques of attack need consideration."

He demanded that Akimu set the example with guile and deception. He stressed humility from Bluff and told him his unreasonable pride would soon get the better of him. Bluff learned this the hard way several times. Epoch suffered defeat (an incredible annoyance to him). Gamba slammed him to the ground during hand-to-hand combat, teaching him that his size and strength would not always protect him. Lunar continued to back off when confronted, so Gamba placed unavoidable obstacles behind him without Lunar's knowledge. "You cannot back away now," he mocked the wimpy-natured white boy.

Then came Ruddy, whom Gamba forced to ask others for help. The Feral Boy found it impossible to complete his tests without a helping hand. And as for Sven, Gamba pitted him against Epoch repeatedly. Some tasks required much more from him. But failure was perhaps the most excellent teacher of all. Sven learned to accept his smallness and use it to his advantage.

All seven failed several times that day. They suffered many obstacles in which they wanted no part. They came to understand that their efforts would often lead to failure. He pushed them to their limits with a stern voice and unwavering gaze. "Failure provides wisdom," he told them.

Gamba demanded nothing but their best. "Men fight not for their survival but for the survival of others. Remember this in your darkest hours."

"It is not the mountain you must conquer, but it is yourself," he announced to them across grounds of dirt and rock. A fire within his eyes burned as bright as the north star upon a moonless night. It inspired the Assemblage, even Haven.

Gamba's training techniques were so grueling and intense that the seven struggled to stand. He drilled them relentlessly, instilling discipline and toughness with each lesson. Though his methods were brutal, his commendation and encouragement strengthened them. They were eager to make him proud.

8

WHAT MAKES A MAN

Each devoured their dinners, desperately needing the nourishment. Immediately after, they competed in conversation, telling gross tales of injuries and bloodshed.

They sang songs and played games. Sven had with him his lyre, which played much like a harp. He plucked a kind melody and sang a soft Norseman tune:

We sail till the end
Valor and pride's intent
A Viking's back to the wind
A Viking's back to the wind
Never give in

Gamba pulled Haven aside and requested they talk. He walked with him down a winding path that led nowhere. The Buccaneer sought to draw out the depths of Haven's heart and what troubled him internally.

"How well do you remember your childhood before Wunduria?" Gamba asked.

"Some," Haven said but quickly admitted, "Not as much as I'd like."

"Tell me what you remember," he requested.

Haven's gaze fixed on the horizon, where the night had claimed it, and fireflies danced in the tall grasses, their light flickering in and out of the blades. His eyes, filled with nostalgia and uncertainty, lingered on the beauty before him. "Both parents raised me. You know, the way it should be. It's just my mother and I here now." His voice trailed off, hinting at a deeper story waiting to be told.

"And your father?"

"From what she told me, he was a brilliant man who loved me very much. But he became sick and did not take care of himself. We had to leave him," Haven explained, his voice tinged with sadness as he looked down at the path below him. "I can remember small moments with him, but I remember more of his presence. But his face." He paused, his expression filled with longing. With a touch of melancholy, Haven admitted, "I can't see it. I don't know what my father looks like."

Gamba responded with a look of shared understanding: "That is a burden no son should bear."

"My memories of him. It's like trying to hold on to the wind." Appropriately, both looked out to the grass that swayed with the breeze. "His sickness was of the mind. It was too dangerous to stay. We left when I was five."

"Is that why you deny the things I teach you?" Gamba asked, "That a man should be capable of terrible things?"

Haven smirked and nodded. "Probably." He then chuckled. "Plus, it is hard for me to deviate from peace. I've believed for so long that peace alone makes a man."

"There is nobility in a peaceful man." Gamba said in a commending tone. "But there is more to a man than that. You must open your mind to that."

"I'm understanding why I should," Haven said, his face softening. "I'm not opposed to your teachings. Please know that," he assuredly said. "From what I know, my father was curious by nature. He was a man of perspective. So, perhaps I should be, too. I'm just hesitant about abandoning what his hopes were for me."

"Which were?"

"To become an example to others. He wanted me to bring peace. To provide a refuge."

"So he named you Haven," Gamba concluded, smiling. "Do you know his name?"

Haven grinned. "Yes, Daniel." He then pouted. "He seems like a dreamer, or he had delusions of grandeur."

"Dreams of a better world are often considered delusions," Gamba replied, increasingly interested in Haven's purpose in life. "I've noticed your talents, Haven. You excel at everything I set before you."

"Yes, I've always been like that. I'm quick to learn and quick to achieve. Most things come naturally. My father was what the outside world calls a scientist. He's a man of knowledge. I believe he played some role in my abilities to thrive."

"A scientist?" Gamba asked.

"We call them scholars in Wunduria, alchemists or inventors." Standing there, gripped by the unknown, Haven closed his eyes. "My mother refuses to talk about him anymore," his voice heightened, and he turned to face Gamba with irritation. "But I want to know more. I want to become the very thing he intended for me. Shouldn't I want that?"

"It is most sons' wishes to honor their father that way."

Haven pulled the green pendant out from under his shirt. "This is all I have from him. See the capsule in the middle?" He lifted the pendant, showing it to Gamba. "My father said it can heal, or it can injure." Haven shook his head. "I don't know what he meant by it."

Gamba browsed it, interested in the contrast to its alleged potential. "Your father offered you a choice. A path to choose—one of pain or healing."

"I've never thought of it that way," he responded, lifting his head to meet Gamba's eyes. "A choice."

"You've never been a father," Gamba smirked.

"Wait, you have children?" he gasped.

"Yes, don't act so surprised," Gamba answered contently. "I have a son and a daughter. I am proud of them both."

Haven smiled and then reflected, looking up at the moon and stars. He tilted his head before speaking. "I want my father to feel that way for me."

An admission Gamba believed to be an essential piece to Haven's inner fears. "Your secret self speaks," he told him.

Haven shrugged, puzzled, returning his necklace under his shirt. "What do you mean?"

"Your great fear; the absence of your father's approval. Without him in your life, you're without a compass, lost in a land that is not yours," Gamba said, looking around at the surrounding land. "That is why you've made yourself a person of peace. You are trying to fulfill your father's wishes. At least what you know of them."

He then put his arm around Haven's shoulder. They started walking back to the others. "Now you are learning to protect peace. You did so for your sheep, but now you will do so for Wunduria. You will provide a refuge for many."

"That's my hope," Haven said.

"You will become a man, with or without his father's guidance. It seems peace is your anchor, but there is more for you to learn."

"What if I fail?" Haven worried.

Gamba shook his head. "The more important question is, what if you don't?"

Haven appreciated the optimism. "You've taught me plenty so far. I haven't figured out what a man is supposed to be, though."

Gamba smiled, happy to hear him admit this. "Oh, that's simple. A man is a child's hero."

This immediately reached his heart, and he looked to Gamba eagerly: "So, I must ask myself, when I think of a hero, what do I see?"

Gamba nodded. "Yes. Envision your hero, then pursue it."

~~~

The fourth day in the Hadza Hills was one of traveling, but one thing remained: a final duel. Haven and Gamba set to duel again, away from the forest's darkness. Their arena was an open green field under blue skies and enormous white clouds. Jehu and the six others stood at a distance, spectating the match under the glorious sun.

With their two swords raised, they circled each other, looking for an opening. Haven's eyes darted around, analyzing Gamba's movements, searching for a weakness. Gamba, too, searched for an advantage; his sword held steady and ready to strike. Suddenly, the crash of metal rang as the two clashed swords.

The weight of Gamba's blade felt heavy against Haven's. The vibrations traveled up the hilt into his arms. His sweat beaded on his forehead as the battle raged on. Each strike became faster and more robust, testing the limits of both combatants. Neither would relent, and their swords became a blur of motion.

The intensity of the fight proved both exhilarating and exhausting. Haven's muscles strained with each swing. He could sense Gamba's strength and determination, and a thrill raced through him each time he blocked a swing. The steel rang in his ears as he stared back into his mentor's eyes.

"I will ask you again, what is a man?" Gamba teased as their swords clanked.

"A man is a hero," Haven answered and soon gained an advantage in position and struck Gamba's jacket, cutting a piece of the shoulder's exterior fabric. Gamba smiled and praised the boy.

The clang of metal furred the other six to cheer louder. Collectively, they chanted their leader's name. "Haven!"

Jehu chuckled, pleased to see such bonding.

Skilled and poised, Gamba lunged forward with precision, his blade flashing in the sunlight. The young man countered each strike eagerly, his movements fueled by an unyielding desire to prove himself.

"But what is a man to you?" Gamba asked. "When you become a man, what will you become?" His slashing quickened, leaving Haven little time to defend. Their movements sped up as their swords clashed in a flurry of rapid exchanges, but Haven's resolve continued. With each parry and thrust, he pushed himself beyond his limits, matching his mentor's prowess with unwavering demands. The mentor, taken aback by the ferocity of his protégé, fought with intensified focus, yet the young man seemed to expect every move.

"I will become a terror!" Haven responded angrily. "I will become both peace and conflict! When I am a man, I will be a refuge for innocence but a nightmare for those who prey on it."

Gamba heightened the stakes. He slashed Haven's shoulder, cutting his clothing and skin. Haven winced, feeling its sting, but he did not cower. He countered the cut with one of his own, slashing Gamba's arm. In a lightning-fast maneuver, Haven spun, disarming his mentor with a calculated precision that left the seasoned warrior momentarily stunned.

"I am your nightmare!" Haven said, pointing his sword at his mentor's neck. The training ground fell silent, and the young man stood, chest heaving.

Gamba found himself swordless. He looked down and discovered his sword on the ground. In that moment, Haven defeated his teacher, beginning a new chapter in his journey as a swordsman and leader. Haven pointed his blade at Gamba, ready to strike. His eyes were wide with expectation. He won the duel.

Gamba surrendered, kneeling to one knee.

His six comrades burst into acclaim: "Hurray! Hurrah! Bravo!"

"You did it, Haven!" Bluff exclaimed, clapping powerfully.

Haven shook his head. His fury disappeared. A new raging determination existed inside him. To accomplish his purpose in this quest, he needed to become whatever was needed.

Haven grabbed his mentor's outstretched hand, lifting him from the ground. Amid the others' cheers, Gamba placed his hand behind Haven's neck and pressed their foreheads together. "You are no longer a shepherd of sheep," Gamba said. "Stand tall. You are a leader of men."

9

CROSSING OVER

They traversed a vast expanse of plains, the horizon stretching endlessly before them. An orange streak of aurora streamed high above them.

As the early afternoon sun beat down, they approached an imposing infantry outpost, its walls rising into the surrounding landscape near the towering Krow's Watchtower. They left their wagon behind, deeming it unnecessary for the journey ahead, and loaded up on provisions, preparing for the challenges that awaited them.

The Hadzian military tailor outfitted each soldier with the available armor. "It is worthy of combat," he assured them repeatedly, inspecting them, tugging at their new outfits, making sure they required no further alterations.

"I look like a true soldier," Ruddy chirped, his voice filled with pride and disbelief. He was no longer draped in his woodland decor but in a proper combat uniform. His dry grass helmet lay behind him on the ground, as he knew it would not protect against the dangers ahead. "This metal helmet is heavy, though," he added, struggling to feel comfortable.

Sven knocked on it and then on his own. "It's inferior to my Vig helmet." He bragged, still wearing his Viking horned helmet, which, by this point, Gamba demanded he leave behind because it was too large for his head.

In response to Sven, Lunar rolled his eyes. "We get it, Sven. Vikings are the epitome of strength. Blah, blah, blah." He taunted, using his hand to mimic a talking mouth.

"At least I have something to be proud of. Pulver is filled with weak boys like you. I'm sure your women still wipe your behinds."

As Lunar secured the final piece of his robust armor, a profound change came over him. His usual fidgety movements stilled, and a smile of genuine self-assurance replaced his usual nervous grin. His voice, usually soft-spoken, carried a new strength as he spoke. "They don't wipe our behinds, you imbecile," He retorted, his gaze unwavering as he met Sven's eyes. "Pulveran women are fair, intelligent, and have earned their place among Pulver's highest courts. Not like your women, who smell and look like pigs."

"How dare you!" Sven erupted, lunging forward with a fiery rage. His face flushed with a deep crimson, and he charged at Lunar. Sensing the impending clash, the others sprang into action, seizing Sven by the shoulders to subdue him. He thrashed and bellowed his fury. "You're the pig!" he spat. Lunar stepped back, his newfound confidence wavering under the power of Sven's wrath.

"Epoch, grab him," Haven's authoritative voice commanded. The Giant lifted the small Viking off the ground and constricted him. He quickly controlled Sven's flailing swings and kicks. Haven's firm and commanding voice cut through the scuffle as he ordered them to stop. "Save your anger for Snarlag," he declared. His words, imbued with a sense of urgent leadership, brought immediate stillness to the group.

Sven, still seething, glared at Lunar, who swallowed hard and nodded in understanding. Epoch lowered Sven to the ground. "Behave, okay," the Tribesman advised with his soothing low tone.

After leaving the outpost with many resources, the seven admired the enhanced stature the copper armor lent them. Their eyes traveled from one to another, exchanging nods of approval and expressions of newfound confidence. Each of them, except for Akimu, who remained in his original garb, gleamed of polished copper metal under the sunlight. Their green gambeson provided a padded layer of protection and was quite flexible. They resembled Hadzian Archers. This would make an enemy think twice before attacking.

Before leaving the outpost, they secured many valuable foods and supplies. Most of which were Hadzian specialties.

Gamba and Jehu rode their horses side by side, their eyes gleaming with pride as they watched the seven young men ride ahead. All nine rode their horses to the northernmost distance of the Hadzian Kingdom. They reached the Osprey Bridge, the only bridge connecting the Hadzian Kingdom with the Neutral Occupancy—a small section of land unowned and valueless by all those in kingdom power.

Built from stone and cedars long ago, the bridge needed repair. No one cared to maintain it, though. The only person who valued the bridge was the Keeper, who lived in the small bridge house. He received compensation from the Royal Guard for his duties. Not that they needed him much. The Hadzian Stealth Rangers protected the land from any intruders. Criminals dared not to test the ranger's ability to patrol the borders. Because of this, Island Defectors never crossed over into Hadzian land, a crime punishable by death.

Gamba and Haven trotted their horses up to the Osprey bridge. The structure's engineers designed it with two large wings at the center. The nine admired the brilliant architecture briefly before attempting to pass it.

Holding a long spear, the Keeper stepped out from his toll booth. He was a fat man and clumsy-looking. He shuffled his way out and stood at the bridge's entrance. "Who goes there?" he called out.

Gamba looked at Haven jocularly. "Who is this fool?" Gamba muttered under his breath. "We need to cross this bridge, good man! Please step aside!"

The Keeper, who went by the name Dulf, shook his head. "Are you deaf? I asked, who goes there?" He held out his spear as if he were a threat to anyone other than himself.

Gamba rolled his eyes. "You've got to be kidding me," he said to Haven. "The king sends us! He tasked us with a most important errand! Please, step aside and allow us to pass!"

Dulf paused momentarily, looking at the group. "How many of you are there?" he asked, unable to count.

"Nine!" Gamba replied frustratedly. "Now, will you allow us to pass?"

Squinting, Dulf thought for a moment but then vigorously shook his head. "No, I do not believe you. You are fugitives on the run. You're trying to trick me!"

"I will not bicker with you," Gamba replied. "Step aside!"

"No!" Dulf shouted. "You can't tell me what to do! I can stand wherever I want!" He then took a few steps to the side. "See! I am standing here now! I can stand wherever I want!" he protested, pounding his feet like a fat toddler.

"What an odd fellow. Maybe he's looking for a bribe?" Haven wondered aloud, turning to Gamba for an answer. But the Buccaneer reached for his sword. Just then, walking past him, was Jehu.

"Let me handle this," he grumbled. "I have a way with simple folk. Geezers have great communicational skills, you know."

Gamba slouched. "Fine. We'll do it your way."

The other six paid close attention, riding their horses closer to Gamba and Haven. They watched Jehu walk over, leaning on his staff for support more than usual. "I think all this traveling has worn the Geezer out. He's too old to travel so far," Lunar said.

Bluff smiled, amused by Lunar's naivety. "I'm not so sure about that."

Jehu approached the Bridge Keeper gingerly, like an old man in his last days. "Young man, I applaud you for your skepticism," He said slowly. "You are to be respected. The king sent us here to test you. Your brave actions are to be praised."

Dulf held his neck up. "Really?" he exclaimed. "You'll tell him how brave I am? Oh, thank you! I've been guarding this bridge most of my life. No one understands how good I am at it. No one ever asks. Just me and the birds out here." He turned around, lifting his pants that sagged past his waist. He looked up at the bridge's wings and the osprey above them. "Yep, I am the only bridge keeper. What would the king do without me?"

Annoyed by the man's blather, Jehu swung his staff and thumped the back of the halfwit's head. Dulf dropped to the ground plumply.

Surprised by Jehu's swift act, Haven's eyes widened. Gamba laughed wholeheartedly. His head leaned back, and his shoulders shook. Sven and Epoch did much the same. Their laughs were genuine, unrestrained expressions of amusement.

Bluff then poked Lunar. "Never block the path of a Geezer. He might be old, but he's still clever."

Impressed with Jehu's strength, Sven and Lunar exchanged amazed glances. "I won't cross that old man's path," Lunar said, chuckling.

Jehu turned around to the others. "There, that wasn't so difficult!" he said happily. "Epoch! Move the man to his little house. Let's pass this place and be done with it."

Gamba clapped his hands. "Jehu, still a scoundrel!"

While the others crossed the bridge without hesitation, Haven lingered. He peered out to the land of San Hadza, a comfortable place he loved dearly. Trepidation rose in his heart. He pondered all he would leave behind and most likely never return to. He thought of his mother, the incredible person she was. She brought him to this lovely land, a place filled with peace and beauty, and he appreciated her dearly for it.

He thought of what Gamba taught him. He struggled to believe he could be the one to preserve the peace. *Will I save this beautiful land?*

"Taking one last look at home?" Bluff asked, looking up at him from the ground.

Haven snapped out of his discontent. "This is the farthest from home I've ever gone." Bluff nodded before looking out at the land. Haven shrugged. "I'm leaving so much behind."

"That is the way of things," Bluff remarked. "The further you go, the more you leave behind. And there's no going back."

Although he agreed with the harsh reality, Bluff's words pierced his heart. "I know there's no going back," he responded. "Fighting Snarlag will cost us our lives."

Sensing Haven's hesitance, Bluff walked toward the bridge, where his horse waited for him. He called out to Haven. "You cherish what's behind you while I run from it!"

Haven smirked. "You coward!"

Bluff chuckled. "I'm the coward? You won't even get on the bridge! I thought you were our leader?"

Appreciating the teasing, Haven trotted Thunder toward the bridge. "You may not always like how I lead!" he shouted mockingly.

Bluff responded in kind. "Rid yourself of this pretty land! You need some ugly in your life!"

"You're all the ugly I need in life, Bluff."

Haven tightened his legs and commanded his horse. "Ride!" Thunder immediately descended into a gallop, speeding past Bluff and onto the bridge.

Thunder rode faster and faster, speeding past the others. By the quickness of his steed, Haven reached the other side first. He couldn't help but laugh excitedly. With renewed motivation, he challenged the others: "Hurry yourselves! We've got a worm to kill!"

The Neutral Occupancy wasn't much to look at. Once across the Osprey Bridge, the green grass and vegetation withered into a barren wasteland. They traveled onto a dry and cracked earth covered with thorns and thistles.

There were many dreadful places to avoid in this land. Black dead trees stood tall, with skeletal branches reaching up to the blazing sun. Gamba knew the road ahead to be dangerous. The surroundings were not hospitable to horses, either. It was an unproductive wilderness filled with rocks, holes, snakes, and scorpions. The silent land felt hollow and lonely.

After some hours of traveling, they saw a town called Pringus. Jehu told the young men they needed to make a brief stop at a tavern that wasn't much out of their way. Despite Pringus being a place of trouble, he promised them it would be worth their time.

Mostly wretched people lived there, like the ill poor folk who spent their days sitting outside their huts and shacks—the closer to Pringus they came, the more civilization they encountered. The seven looked around at the people and mud buildings.

"Bleak," Sven said.

Many vagabonds thrust their items toward the seven, trying to sell whatever they could. Jehu and Gamba scared them off as soon as they became too intrusive. Haven felt pity for them, even though they were nasty people who were harsh with words. They soon saw Wolf Herders from the Fierk Forest, too, but passed them quickly out of precaution.

There were also the Ravings and Barmys who, like dogs barking at the unknown, shouted insults at any man who passed by their encampment. Most were blue-haired Bull Women, a wickedly angry bunch who sought conflict. These were fat and ugly women who, at the moment, threw mud at the nine for passing by.

"You are the reason we die here!" they shouted. "You hate us! You oppress us!"

Their accusations bothered the seven young men a great deal. Gamba responded by telling his students to ignore every word the women said and not reply to their madness. But as Haven saw their crooked behaviors, he spoke to them sincerely: "We do not hate you." Rather than listening to him, they screeched in pain and shook as if having a seizure.

Sven shouted, "We are not here to hurt you!" But the Bull Women continued to shriek. Gamba yelled out at the seven, commanding them to quicken their pace. He'd much rather deal with the thieves and abusers of Pringus than these bitter, unreasonable women.

Before reaching Pringus, Gamba rode alongside the seven. He advised them: "Beware the woman when you speak truth; it will break her heart."

As Gamba returned to the front of their caravan, Bluff called out to him, "If truth breaks a woman's heart, what breaks a man's?"

Gamba replied, "Lies."

What some would consider an offensive slight, Bluff understood to be a lesson in a man's use of communication. Gamba's words did not disparage women but distinguished men and their duty to be instruments of truth.

They then reached their destination. Jehu put on a happy face, but he was not blind to the condemnable nature of Pringus and its locals. The tavern he intended to visit remained the disgusting dive he knew it to be. The smell worsened the closer they came to it. The Juxtus Inn and Pub lived up to its reputation. The seven young ones heard stories about it through the years. It was exactly as they heard it to be; a stomping ground for scum and drunkards.

As they neared the pub, Gamba warned them, "Keep your heads down and your eyes to yourselves. We are not welcome here." The seven took the warning seriously. Sven, however, scoffed as if he were ready for a scuffle.

Haven remained alert. When asked again about the visit, Jehu replied, "To repay an old friend."

Right outside the pub's entrance sat a dirty man who lived without wits. He stunk of a foul smell, and drool dripped down his chin. He laughed with nearly every breath he took. He wore a crown on top of his soggy hair, which, at close inspection, dripped with a syrupy substance.

The man's crown, crafted from some cheap metal, had symbols on the front which, in the ancient native language, read "King Laughter." Gamba and Jehu ignored the miscreant while the seven walked past him nervously. They each stepped into the pub with mixed emotions.

Epoch entered with an imposing presence that commanded immediate attention from the miscreants near the entrance. He moved with a silent and thunderous confidence, eliciting respect from the criminals that occupied the place.

As he stepped further into the tavern, a hush fell over those he passed by, their earlier bravado wilting under the shadow of his size. Epoch's mere presence parted the crowd of lawless ones. There wasn't enough beer or liquor in all of existence to convince any scum to stand in the Giant's way.

The establishment reeked of decaying meat, causing Lunar to run outside and vomit as King Laughter laughed on. "The greater our churl, the bigger the hurl!" He cackled.

As disgusting of a place as it was, those who occupied it were even worse. It was an overcrowded mess filled with greasy men drinking pints of beer and savagely ripping apart meat with their teeth. If these scum felt the urge to spit, they did so onto the floor without hesitation. Two grotesque individuals arm wrestled, grunting like wild pigs. Others shouted out and wagered money on the victor. Every sort of villain occupied the pub. Too curious to keep their heads down, the seven young men looked up briefly as they followed Gamba. They saw the Faceless Ones, the Ugly Truth, the Red Riln, the infamous Dredger, and others who were legends of crime.

Gamba Tru, unbothered by it all, led the way toward a table near the bar. Some recognized him and slouched back out of fear. Jehu followed the group from behind.

Looking around the tavern, Gamba sized up every individual he could see. He reviewed the pub layout, where every window was, and every escape route. A behavior he learned in his youth—taught to him by his father and older brother. And, of course, he learned it the hard way.

"This place hasn't changed a bit," Gamba muttered before he turned to the seven. "Remember, keep your eyes to yourselves."

Sven whispered to Lunar, "Don't look at anyone, or you'll get us killed."

"If anyone gets us killed, it'll be me," Gamba remarked as he looked around the pub for familiar faces. "I've spotted two ex-bucs who'd like to see me dead. I'm sure there are others."

"I might throw up again," Lunar warned.

Sven rolled his eyes. "Toughen up." Lunar dropped his head to the table, covering it with his arms.

Turning to Jehu, Haven asked a most fraught question. "Jehu, I know you explained earlier, but why are we here?"

Jehu replied kindly, "To see someone who may help us with needed materials. We won't be long. Do not fear."

A fat waitress skipped to the table, compromising the group's discreet presence. "Look who we got here—Gamba Tru! The man who broke my heart!" she shouted for the entire pub to hear. "You've got guts showing your Pirate face here. Clunker over there would like to stick a knife through your heart. He wants to do it," she yapped, pointing at a large fellow at the bar who stared at Gamba with contempt. "But I told him no."

"I don't need your protection," Gamba said with a sneering grin.

She returned his grin with one of her own, which bore a snaggletooth through her lips. "Oh, I think you do, Pirate. Seeing that you still owe my father plenty of Red Beryl."

"Ain't that nice of you to remind me?" He chirped back.

She played with her blonde hair, twirling it at the ends. "You better have my father's gems. He's not the forgiving man he once was."

"Enough with your reminders, woman," Gamba moaned. "You're not as endearing as I remember you to be."

She smiled and puckered her lips. "You know, if you were to maybe, oh, I don't know, make me your wife. I could persuade him to forgive your debt altogether," she insinuated with a wink. Her blonde hair flowed down her back and shoulders, and her low-cut top left little to the imagination. She was a prize to the brutal men that surrounded her, but to any decently minded man, she lacked civility. Her face, plastered with every sort of cosmetic, oozed with beads of sweat. She decorated her massive arms with tattoos. She stunk of sweat, and her apron needed a good wash, as did every other garment she wore. "What do you think, hun? Make me your wife?" she asked affectionately, leaning into him.

"I'd rather your father kill me," he replied with a wink.

She stiffened and stomped her foot. "You fool, Gamba Tru," she scolded. "The second he sees you, every henchman he's got will draw their knives. They'll cut you open—"

"Miley!" a raspy voice shouted from a staircase beside the bar. "Get back to work!" It was her father, Juxtus Lunder. The very man Gamba owed a fortune to. An old debt that even Gamba knew would eventually cost him his life if never paid.

Juxtus Lunder limped over to the table. He was short but tall with malevolence, old as Jehu but grittier. Juxtus was the owner of the inn and pub for nearly fifty years. With each passing decade, the reputation worsened. Juxtus was a dirtbag of a man who conned any person he could. All of Wunduria knew his ways to be devious. He had a robust network with every sinister foe on the island. His place of business acted as an asylum for the guilty. The old scum favored that type of person. His voice was scruff, like his behavior and appearance.

"Gamba Tru. A Pirate if I'd ever see one." Juxtus announced.

Buccaneers considered the term Pirate to be an offensive thing. The Buccaneers of the East were nothing like Pirates, or so they say. Juxtus laughed, wheezing through a heavy cough, almost proud of the Buccaneer's bad reputation. "Are you here to pay me that treasure of mine? Or shall I kill you now?"

He walked with a heavy limp toward their table. His white mustache and beard were much whiter than Gamba ever remembered. But it had been many years since their last interaction.

"You killed the last two bounty hunters I sent your way," Juxtus accused, leaning against the table.

"Oh right, I apologize for that, Lunder. I do enjoy living," Gamba replied. "Plus, I didn't kill them. They died from their own stupidity."

"You know how much I enjoy your lethal antics. We should drink rum and share our stories of crime. But you pester me, you ghastly Spaniard. I want my red beryls," Juxtus responded. His two henchmen, Tweeds and Deets, stood tall behind him. They glared at Gamba, wanting to kill him, though they couldn't even if they tried.

Haven reached for his blade, assuming a fight was inevitable. Jehu placed his hand over it, preventing him from drawing it.

"Easy, lad," Jehu cautioned.

Despite his poor eyesight, Juxtus caught sight of Jehu sitting at the table. Juxtus's tone lightened a moment when speaking to the Geezer. "It's a pity to see you here, Jehu, sitting with a Pirate. I never thought I'd see you with such savagery."

"Time changes many things, old friend. You and I know that well," Jehu remarked. Juxtus nodded, seeing Jehu's kind glare.

"Lunder, we should talk privately," Gamba interrupted.

"Why?" he prodded, angered easily. "So I can kill you without an audience? Give me my red beryls!"

"Don't be hasty. I want to negotiate the debt I owe you."

"Negotiate? What for? How many pieces I cut your body up into?"

Tweeds and Deets walked over to Gamba. They were indeed fit contenders, ready and willing to fight. They clenched their fists for a brawl, sneering at the Buccaneer.

"Well, this has escalated quickly," Jehu piped in, ready to involve himself in this quarrel.

Tweeds and Deets' encroachment provoked Epoch to stand, placing himself between Gamba and the two henchmen. He pushed Gamba behind him and growled at his new opponents, ready to grapple. Haven put his hand back to his blade. As for Lunder, he took a step back, shocked by the size of the young brown Tribesman.

"Dear heavens, what do we have here?" Juxtus gasped, staring up at the Giant. Impressed by his form and willingness to fight, Juxtus looked at Gamba and smiled. "Perhaps we should talk in private."

"Don't do it," Haven whispered.

Gamba peeked around Epoch's arm at Jehu. "Your turn, old man."

Jehu nodded and stood up. "There will be no need for that, Justice," Jehu added, calling Juxtus by his true name. Jehu stood up from the table and took a small brown pouch out of his pocket. He then tossed it to him.

"What is this?" Juxtus asked, catching it quickly. He held the pouch up and examined it.

"A gift," Jehu said kindly. "The Lion sends his regards."

Juxtus stiffened, and his face grew pale. "The Lion?" he muttered, peering at Jehu in disbelief.

Hearing him utter that title, the bar grew eerily quiet. Every man shut up and looked in Juxtus' direction. Miley's face froze, too. His henchmen backed away. With such a gracious tone, Jehu spoke consolingly to Juxtus.

"He wanted to deliver it to you personally, but an emergency prevented him from doing so. He apologizes for the delay in its delivery. If it were within his power, he would have brought it to you sooner," Jehu explained.

Gamba was unaware of the pouch's contents. Jehu had only told him that the contents were of great value and would eliminate his significant debt. However, like the seven young men, Gamba grew curious about what was inside the pouch and why every criminal in the tavern became silent at hearing the title "The Lion."

Juxtus Lunder opened the pouch to peek inside. His daughter Miley looked at him with anticipation. After seeing its contents, Juxtus pressed the bag to his chest. He choked up a bit, and his eyes watered. He fell back, but his henchmen caught him. He collected himself and barked some orders to them. The two henchmen ran away and up the staircase.

Juxtus spoke kindly: "Thank you, Jehu, son of Alden." Looking up at him, he said sincerely, "You know what this means to me, Jehu. Words cannot express my gratitude."

Jehu smiled. "All the Lion requests is that you forgive Gamba his heavy debt." Gamba and the seven young men looked on in amazement. Haven no longer reached for his blade. *What's inside the pouch?*

Juxtus walked over to the staircase, pressing the pouch against his chest. "I cancel your debt, Pirate," he said calmly. "If you'll excuse me, I have personal matters to attend to," he sputtered. He limped his way upstairs, as happy as he'd ever been. Tears dripped down his face.

"Give my love to Linda," Jehu requested.

Juxtus paused a moment and turned to him. "Thank you, old friend." And away he went.

"Whatever was in that pouch just saved my life," Gamba confessed. "Juxtus Lunder has a heart, after all."

Jehu nodded with a gentle smile. "Even the angriest men have a heart, Gamba. His doesn't sit in his chest. It belongs to another."

Gamba wasn't sure what to make of it, but the relief of his canceled debt was enough for him to show a grateful smile.

"What's inside the pouch?" Haven asked quietly.

Jehu looked at him and replied, "A second chance."

10

CAVE TROUBLE

The next day, bright and early, Juxtus's two henchmen presented each of the seven with various medicines and balms for their journey. "Consider it a parting gift," Tweeds and Deets said.

"You will no doubt need these. Safeguard them, lads." Jehu admonished.

Gamba led the group north towards a boundary that marked the passage into uncharted lands, like the enigmatic Bitrs Cavus, a labyrinth of confusing caves.

Haven couldn't help but inquire about the mysterious Lion individual spoken of earlier. Jehu explained, "I will reveal the truth about the Lion soon. It is a weighty matter. I must explain it delicately, but I do not yet know how."

After a brisk ride out, they reached a long strip of pines. There, they rode their horses along a soft and clean path. The tall trees provided pleasing shade while many squirrels scurried about. There were also deer, which roamed about eating the pine seeds and small patches of forbs.

Ruddy felt most at peace among the seven. He sat on his horse quietly, with his head down and eyes closed, listening to the sounds of the wildlife. As they traveled, he'd dismount his horse to gather different flowers and herbs, placing them into separate jars.

"What are those?" Haven asked him.

"Plants with particular residues. Just following a hunch," he stated.

They came to a momentary halt and allowed their horses to feed at a patch of alfalfa. Seated beside a mound of dirt, Ruddy sprinkled pieces of the particular plants into the soil. The mixture had a captivating effect, attracting earthworms to the surface.

Ruddy's smile broadened, his eyes alight with success, for he believed he had unlocked a secret. Using this blend of particular flowers and herbs, a secret known only to those who speak the language of the wild, he had called to these insects, inviting them to the surface. "Just gotta know how to talk to 'em," he said.

He removed his helmet. His mess of red hair glowed like the embers of a dying fire under the pine canopy. A smile played across his lips, and his cheeks flushed.

"I will collect more of these plants," Ruddy said, standing up from the mound of dirt. "If my hunch proves true, it may lead to greater things." He brushed the dirt off his hands. "If Snarlag is anything like a worm, we might appeal to her senses."

Haven agreed, admiring his friend's way of thinking. They continued their blissful ride through the strip of pines, which led them to the caves. Ruddy whistled for a finch as they approached, and one landed on his finger. He gave it a tiny seed, but the bird bit him before flying off. "Ouch," he complained.

Jehu leaned into him. "From here on out, do not trust innocence, my young Ruddy. The closer you get to the mountains, the more peaceful things will betray you."

Gamba snapped his fingers to get everyone's attention. "These caves contain half-truths and lies. Do not trust them."

Each had their inklings of what to expect, primarily tricks and shams. Maybe poisonous spiders were hanging about, or slithering things hid in dark corners. When they rode to the first cave, the opposite was quite true.

The entrance was inviting and well-maintained. Inside, a staircase led up very high. Vibrant plants ran along each side, as did trees with delightful flowers. Sunlight shone through the cave's roof and illuminated the beauty within.

"It's gorgeous!" Lunar said with relief. Unnoticed by Gamba, Lunar dismounted his horse and ran toward the cave's entrance. Inside, the stairs led up to an immense opening. "There's a doorway! You can see the light at the end of the tunnel," he said gleefully. Without hesitation, he ran toward the cave's entrance. "I can smell the honeysuckle!"

But upon noticing Lunar's foolishness, Gamba took action. "No, Lunar!" He reached for his grapple and flung it at the boy's legs. It captured him around the ankles, and Gamba pulled with immense force, yanking him to the ground.

"What are you doing?" Haven cried out.

But Gamba did not reply. He let the cave's trap speak for itself.

Lunar's first step into the cave triggered a deathly trap. A guillotine's blade dropped from a crack above and landed on the cave's floor. It was so sharp it pierced the ground and stuck there. They gasped loudly.

Jehu ran toward the boy, who had hit the ground abruptly. Gamba looked up through the trees above him and sighed. Though hurt, Lunar lay there, safe from the guillotine's blade.

He rolled over in pain, with a bloody nose to match. He pinched it, moaning. Jehu pulled a scarf from his pocket and handed it to the boy.

"You saved his life," Haven uttered.

"A fool rushes in where he ought not," Gamba replied.

"My ankles!" Lunar cried with the grapple wrapped around them tightly.

"Bluff, his ankles will be soar. Help him relieve his pain," Gamba ordered. Bluff nodded, searching through the balms they had received earlier.

As Gamba retrieved his grapple, Jehu guided Lunar back to the others. The Pulveran limped as he walked, and his ankles dripped with blood. He held his head back, pinching his nose shut with Jehu's scarf.

"When your nose stops bleeding, treat your ankles," Jehu instructed, shaking his head, bothered by the boy's foolishness. "You can keep the scarf."

"I almost died," Lunar said in a nasal voice as he returned to the group.

Gamba addressed the young men in his usual authoritative voice. He emphasized what he already told them, "I told you the Bitrs are not what they appear. Thanks to Lunar's stupidity, you've seen your first example of it. Many have fallen victim to this cave in particular."

They peered into the cave's entrance, understanding what Gamba meant by half-truths and lies.

"Where are the dead bodies?" Sven asked.

"Hmm?" Gamba responded.

"If people die here, there should be remains. You know, skulls and stuff," he continued, lifting his head with intrigue. "One cannot go inside to retrieve them, lest they trigger another trap."

"There are keepers to these caves," Gamba explained. "The last of the natives to this land—the Xynd." A chill fell upon the seven young ones.

"The Xynd?" Bluff whispered.

They knew not to disturb the Xynd. This was an unlawful act agreed upon by every kingdom in Wunduria. "These caves are neutral grounds that separate their nation from any other. They do not take kindly to strangers who enter it. If they find us, they will kill us," Gamba warned sternly. "The Xynd are never to be underestimated."

Rumors swirled among the neighboring lands regarding the natives' rituals and the fierce guardianship of their territory, which was said to be protected by ingenious snares. Travelers of Wunduria spoke in low tones of those who ventured too close and never returned from the jungles the Xynd occupied.

Something rather unexpected occurred before the seven could worry too much about it. A crow flew down from the trees and perched on Jehu's shoulder. The young men looked at one other, amazed. However, Gamba and Jehu knew precisely what the crow's arrival meant. The Geezer lowered his head, and a worried complexion fell over his face.

"You've traveled a great distance, haven't you, Sammy?" he said to the bird. The crow leaned into him and cawed. A red ribbon was tied to the crow's leg, causing Jehu to frown further.

"Jehu, what's with the crow?" Ruddy asked. But the Geezer did not reply.

"Something awful has happened," Gamba answered.

"This is most unfortunate," Jehu admitted. Sadly, he told the Assemblage, "I have arranged a Skyship to meet us." He paused and corrected himself, "To meet you on the other side. My brother, Shumi, is the pilot. He will carry you as far as the wind will take him."

"Can't he pick us up here?" Lunar asked, still pinching his nose with the scarf. Bluff clocked him in the head with his red staff. "Ow!" Lunar whined.

Haven stepped forward. "I take it the crow is a messenger?"

"That is correct, lad," Jehu said, lowering his head. "The crow is a signal. I am needed elsewhere immediately."

"Elsewhere?" Haven asked anxiously.

"You're leaving us?" Epoch worried, his shoulders slumping forward.

"I must ride east to the Palelands," Jehu explained. "The Castle of Hills requires my attention. This is not a call I can ignore."

But Haven protested, "You can't just leave us. You're the one who called us on this quest."

Jehu mounted his horse. "I am sorry, my boy, but I must."

"You know this because of a crow?" Haven griped, pointing at the bird.

Just then, a raven flew down through the trees and onto Gamba's shoulder. They looked at him nervously and saw a purple ribbon tied to the raven's leg.

"You too?" Jehu said to Gamba.

Lifting his axe, Sven growled, "I'll kill the next bird I see."

The Buccaneer cursed loudly and then announced the unfortunate truth. "I must leave, too."

"You're both leaving? You can't!" Haven protested, his voice raised and his hands clenched to his sides.

"But we've come so far!" Bluff rasped.

Mounted on his horse, Gamba shouted to the young men, "Yes, I know, but there is a parlay I must meet." He then turned toward Haven. "My leaving you was inevitable after I showed you the way through the caves. I do not wish to leave you this way, but the Assemblage is yours to lead now. This is what I trained you for."

Gamba reached into his pocket and removed a folded paper wrapped in string. He tossed it to Bluff, who was closest to him. "This map reveals the correct course through the caves. Follow each direction. It will mean your lives," Gamba warned. "Reach the summit. When you hear the horns of Tortuga Nue, look to the east. I'll be there, and I'll expect to find you. Remember this: it is not the mountain you must conquer, but it is yourself." Gamba then turned his horse, ready to depart. "Haste!" he commanded. And just like that, he left, disappearing into the trees.

The seven stood there, trying to grasp what had just occurred. They turned their attention to Jehu, who steadied his horse.

"You must reach the summit," he said to Haven. "Once you are there, find the Lion. I consider him trustworthy, and so should you. He is the reason I searched for you. He is the one who told me you can tame the earthquake."

"Why did you wait to tell me this?" He implored.

"There is more I intended to tell you. But you must be ready to hear it." Jehu steadied his horse for departure, grasping the reins firmly. "Promise me you'll find this man."

Haven hesitated, mostly confused.

"Promise me!" Jehu urged him.

This shocked Haven into a response. "Yes, I promise."

"The time we have is now reduced," Jehu warned. "I must go!" Before galloping off, the Geezer cast a lingering look over his shoulder at the young men, his expression bittersweet. He was so very proud of his seven young friends. "You will be heroes," he assured them.

He commanded his horse and fled into the unknown, disappearing into the trees like Gamba had.

"He left us," Haven muttered.

After complete silence, the Assemblage dismounted their horses to join Bluff and Lunar on the ground. They all stood there quietly, looking at one another. As their initial shock wore off, Bluff spoke out frustratedly. "The time we have is now reduced?"

Akimu's expression deepened with sorrow. His usually neutral demeanor gave way to visible despair, a rare crack in his martial stoicism.

Haven's hurried and frenzied footsteps ceased when he noticed his comrades' bewildered and apprehensive expressions. The burden of leadership weighed heavily on his mind. He tried to calm himself by placing his hand over his chest, feeling his green pendant necklace.

Taking a deep breath, he knew he had to lead by example and reassure his team that they could overcome any obstacle. He lifted his head high, facing them with confidence. His shoulders squared, and his gaze sharpened. He stepped forward. His firm voice broke the silence.

"It appears we have little time—less than we thought. We're at the tipping point, and there is nowhere to go but forward. We must reach the summit," Haven instructed. "We are more than the sum of our anxieties," he declared, his words weaving an influence of courage around them.

Their postures subtly shifted as he spoke, imitating the change they observed in him.

Haven stood tall, staring back at them. "Epoch, son of Mammonthal. Sven, son of Gorl. Bluff, son of Darius. Lunar, son of Skyth. Ruddy, son to Connor. And Akimu, son to the Shadow Flame. Do you commit your way to me and each other?" he asked urgently.

They each nodded and confirmed. "Yes."

Haven lifted his crook. "As I told you at the outset, I am Haven, the shepherd who will guide you safely through danger because failure has no hold on me."

They held their chins high, ready to continue forward. "We will follow you," they said in unison, finding themselves burgeoning bravery, ready to face the unknown as a united front.

"Now, let's find our way through these caves," Haven ordered.

~ ~ ~

Before they could mount their horses, an earthquake shook the ground beneath them.

"Drop to the ground now!" Haven shouted. "Raise your shields over you!"

Reacting with impressive speed, the seven young warriors threw themselves to the ground as the earth convulsed beneath them. They held their shields aloft, creating a protective barrier. The rumbling ground set off a cacophony of creaks and groans in the surrounding pine trees, whose branches thrashed violently, snapping to the ground in a terrifying crash.

The sudden turmoil frightened their horses, who panicked and galloped away. Their powerful hooves kicked up clouds of dust as they disappeared. Thunder, Haven's loyal stallion, remained, moving to stand over them as a protector.

A tree collapsed to the ground beside them, and the entrance to the cave collapsed in on itself, triggering more traps. Many blades flew out from the collapsing entrance.

"Keep your heads down!" Haven shouted.

The shaking slowly subsided, and the Assemblage rose to their feet, except for Lunar, who was in desperate straits. "I hate this place," he whined.

"Get up, you wuss," Sven barked, his voice filled with annoyance.

Haven patted Thunder on the neck. "Thank you, my friend," he said, touching its snout. "My brave stallion."

"Our horses?" Sven asked, looking around.

"They ran off," Ruddy answered. "We didn't tether them to anything. Let's go find 'em."

"Can someone get my horse?" Lunar whined. "My ankles hurt! I can't walk."

"I'll get it, you baby!" Sven shouted as he ran off down the path.

Before retrieving his horse, Bluff handed the map to Haven, who eagerly opened it, his eyes scanning the ancient markings. The words, faded and filled with unfamiliar symbols, were in a language he couldn't decipher. It was a puzzle, a mystery waiting to be solved, and Haven was determined to unravel its secrets.

The others returned with their horses one by one. As an act of goodwill, Sven returned with his and Lunar's, a gesture Sven bragged about to his injured Pulveran comrade.

Acting as their leader, Haven knew to prepare his comrades for travel. "Check your supplies and mount your horses. Plenty of danger lies ahead of us," he told them. He then took Bluff aside.

"You know the language of the Buccaneers, don't you?" he asked.

Under the shade of the pines, Bluff nodded. "Some of it, yes."

Haven handed him the map. "So you can read this?"

Bluff looked it over briefly. "Isn't much of a map? Looks like instructions."

"Can you read it?" Haven asked with a heightened voice, checking to ensure the other five were busy preparing their horses and bags.

"No, not at all. Looks ancient. It's not Buccaneer," he claimed.

"What do you mean? We have to follow what it says."

Bluff shook his head. "I know. But I can't read it. From what I can tell, it's the lost language of the Xynd. And I definitely can't read that."

Haven's eyebrows lowered as he squinted. "You're kidding me. But Gamba gave the map to you," he replied sharply.

"So?" Bluff replied, shrugging his shoulders and curling his lip.

"I thought that meant you knew how to read it," he snapped. "Why else would he give it to you?"

"I was closest to him," he said.

"How are we supposed to read it?" Haven wondered, looking to the others who were almost prepared for travel.

"I don't know. Ask Akimu." Bluff countered. "Maybe he'll know. He is a Flame Shadow. Don't they know the secrets of Wunduria?"

Haven shrugged. "They are protectors of the land, not wise men."

Ruddy trotted over on his horse. "What does the map say?"

Bluff smirked and looked at Haven. "Yeah, what does the map say?" he asked tauntingly, offering the map back.

Haven gave him a dirty look before grabbing it. Too proud to admit he did not know, he smiled as if all was fine and good. "Just follow me!" He said. "I know the way."

"Oh, this should be fun," Bluff remarked. "You better learn to read Xynd fast, or we're lost," he teased, mounting his horse, trying not to laugh. "Haven knows the way, everyone!"

He smiled at Bluff with great disdain. After mounting Thunder, he whispered into its ear, "I have no clue what I'm doing, boy." He rode Thunder out ahead of the rest.

The Assemblage followed Haven in a line, passing many cave entrances, some narrow, some spacious with gardens. One had a brick road, others rocky and jagged.

With every cave they passed by, Haven's doubt grew exponentially. But along the way, they found a small cottage. A well-maintained and welcoming one. They all noticed smoke rising from its chimney. Shortly after, a burly man came out with a long, thick mustache curled at the ends. He greeted them all with a smile.

"Hey there, travelers!" he chuckled. "What brings you young men out this way? I get little company out here." Before Haven could respond, the man answered his own question. "Lookin' for passage through these caves, aren't ya?"

"Why, yes, sir, how did you know?" Haven asked, hoping the man knew how.

"You're not here to see me. I know that for sure. That leaves the Blue Cave as the only reason. After all, why else would a group of travelers with swords and shields travel this close to the native nation? You must be up to something serious."

"We are on a most important quest," Haven stated. "Do you know where this Blue Cave is?" he asked, trying not to express his excitement.

"I thought you knew where the cave was?" Bluff remarked.

"Shut up," he hissed over his shoulder.

"Oh, I know where it is. It's the only safe way through these caves—a labyrinth of secrets, tricks, and surprises that'll cost ya your head. Only one cave will sneak you past those dangers."

Haven dismounted his horse. "We'd love for you to lead us to this place. You might be the last kind soul we see for some time."

The man smiled and giggled. "Sure thing! Let me get my walking stick."

As the burly man hurried off to his home, Bluff whispered to Haven, "Wow. Saved by the man with the long mustache."

He returned quickly with his walking stick and a large bag over his shoulder. "My name is Wally Russ. If you care to know." He counted the seven of them. "Let me see. We have a Norseman, a Pulveran, a Giant, and...heck. I have no clue what the rest of you are."

"We are an odd assortment, aren't we?" Haven acknowledged, wanting to hurry to the cave's entrance.

Wally smiled. "I love the odd ones."

"I apologize, sir, but we are short on time. Will you lead us to the cave?" Haven asked.

"Oh, yes. Sorry, like I said, I don't get many visitors out here," he replied. "Follow me. Be prepared, however. This cave belongs to the Xynd, and they don't like visitors."

So they ventured to the Blue Cave. Wally Russ led the way, speaking the entire time and telling stories of this and that.

Upon seeing the entrance to the cave, they became overwhelmed by its beauty. A waterfall fell from the mountains, feeding water into a small pond. The clear waters reflected the white stone of the rocks above. Evergreens surrounded the pond and continued down it. A stream exited the pond and disappeared into the woods behind them. The soft blue glow of the spring illuminated the cave's entrance. And yet, a darker blue glowed from inside.

"Remarkable," Ruddy commented, gawking at the serene view.

"Yep, that's why I call it the Blue Cave. I've never seen a blue quite like it." Wally added.

"It looks too good to be true," Lunar said.

"Perhaps that's the point," Bluff insinuated. "The first cave was just that—inviting but deadly. Every cave after that has either looked too safe or dangerous—nothing in between."

"Wise insight for a young man," Wally commended. "This cave contains burdens, as well. And the natives visit it often. I suggest you move through it quickly. I have a deal with them that protects me, but if they find newcomers, they will not show mercy."

Ruddy had dismounted and walked toward the entrance. He peered inside. "It drops inside!" he shouted. "But after that, it's open and clear. And the walls are like nothing I've ever seen!" he shouted to the others.

"Your horses will be no good beyond this point," Wally informed them. "This cave is the correct way through, but the beauty wears off—rough footing with a declining roof and an inclining, jagged rocky floor. You'll have to crawl at a certain point. Your Giant might not even fit."

Epoch dismounted his horse and defended himself. "I will fit. I have to."

"Suit yourself." Wally smiled.

"Leave... our horses behind?" Haven stammered. "Are you sure?"

"Don't worry, lad. I will take good care of them. I have plenty of good feed. They will join my colt in its pen. It is a good shelter, I promise you."

Haven dismounted, and then the rest did as well. He placed his head on Thunder's snout. "Stay with Wally, my friend. This man will watch you until this is all over." He pressed his face to Thunder's snout. "Be safe."

Appearing to understand, Thunder snorted and bumped his head against Havens.

"I don't like it either," he replied before giving Thunder over.

Wally gave Haven a bag of tricks, which comprised old grenades collected over the years from outside worldly sources. Wally didn't know what they all did but guessed they could help in dangerous situations. He then gave farewell advice: "Remember, get in fast and move quickly. Don't stop until you reach the other side."

While Wally led all the horses back to his home, the seven entered the cave. They needed to lighten their load since they could not carry as much without their horses, so their horses left with some bags still intact. As they hiked into the cave, Haven led the way, trying to hide his discontent. In his mind and heart, he cursed himself for leaving Thunder behind.

Once inside, a beautiful distraction gave him a reason to pause. The cave walls shined a blue color. Glow snails and slugs clung to them. These insects left behind an unusual radiant slime, which the Pearl Rock walls absorbed. A blue beauty that left them all mesmerized. Even Lunar marveled at the glow. He came from a land where nearly all the surroundings glimmered and blossomed with color. His skin's glow was nothing compared to the magnificent blue surrounding them.

Ruddy picked up some glowing rocks. He tossed one to Bluff and then one to Haven. "Let's keep some. We might need a night light at some point," he said.

"But I'm your nightlight," Lunar remarked, who still walked with a limp.

"Aww, how sweet," Sven mocked. "Lunar is our nightlight."

"Shut up," he replied.

With the cave's entrance far behind them, Haven suggested they quicken their pace. As they did, they walked up to a cliff, which stopped them in their tracks. There before them lay a wide crack—much too wide to jump. On the other side, the cave led into blackness. Akimu dropped a glowing rock down into the crack. Eventually, the darkness swallowed it whole. They never heard it hit bottom, either.

Sven looked over at Akimu. "You know, you're so quiet I sometimes forget you're with us."

Akimu nodded.

"So what is this? A split or a rift?" Lunar asked.

They all peered down into it. "I think it's an abyss," Ruddy estimated.

"A canyon?" Bluff asked.

"Whatever it is, we need to get beyond it," Haven advised. "Epoch, do you think you can jump it?"

Epoch looked over and past it. "No," he admitted.

"Hmm, any suggestions?" Haven asked, inspecting the area. "Maybe use a rope and grapple?" Noticing no one responding, he turned to his comrades. To his disappointment, he saw Sven peeing into the rift.

"I gotta go somewhere," Sven said defensively.

"Brilliant idea! Pee break!" Lunar remarked.

A few of them chuckled. Epoch felt the urge to do the same. So he did just that. "Pee time," he boomed.

Haven looked over at Bluff and Akimu, who both shrugged and agreed. Eventually, all of them peed into the chasm. "Hopefully, there's no one down there," Lunar joked.

"My stream goes the farthest," Sven claimed.

"No way, mine does!" Epoch replied. No one challenged him.

Their joking was short-lived, however. As they chuckled, a sudden breeze came from behind them. A flurry of arrows shot past their heads, sending them into a frenzy. They heard a chant behind them toward the cave's entrance: "Hubah! Zu!"

They turned to find dozens of natives entering the cave and charging right toward them. The cavekeepers found them, and they were furious to find seven trespassers.

"They found us!" Haven cried out. "It's the Xynd!"

11
SURVIVE!

D ressed in green-leafed native wear, hoods and all, the Xynd fired arrows from their bows. Some shot needles using blowguns. Others threw spears.

Sven raised his shield just in time as a series of needles pierced into it in rapid succession. The metallic clink and scrape of the needles piercing his shield alerted the others to grab theirs. Trapped against the chasm, they did not know how to escape.

"What do we do?" Ruddy shouted, holding his shield in front of himself.

Haven looked across the divide. "Lunar! Can we swing across with your grapple?"

"Maybe!" Lunar guessed.

"Show them that glowing body of yours!" Sven proposed. "They might think you're holy!"

Desperate for ideas, Haven thought of Epoch's strength. "Epoch, do you think you can throw us across?"

Epoch kneeled behind his shield, which only covered half his body. He shouted a low, rumbling confirmation.

"Start with Lunar and Ruddy! Throw them across! Then work your way toward me," Haven ordered. Ruddy had pierced his shield into the ground. Behind it, he crouched and used his sling to return shots at the Xynd. He slung several pellets at them, but the distance was great, and they were moving targets. Lunar threw rocks, which proved ineffective. Akimu did the same. His aim was much better, knocking several to the ground.

The natives continued charging, firing their arrows at impressive speeds. They chanted their attack cry. "Hubah! Zu!" Epoch hurried over to Lunar. He stood exposed, with his upper body entirely above their shields while the arrows shot past him.

Without caution, Epoch hurled Lunar across the expanse with a primal roar. Lunar's glowing form traced an arc against the darkness over the chasm. Time slowed to a crawl as the arrows closed in, their deadly tips glinting with danger.

Lunar's skin glistened brightly as he entered the darkness on the other side. He landed on the other side with a thud. The arrows passed over him. Like a spotlight, his face illuminated the dark cave beyond him.

The arrows continued. Several pierced into their shields. The Xynd charged forward. "We need to stop them!" Bluff shouted. "They'll be on us soon!"

Akimu pulled a random grenade from the bag Wally Russ had given them.

"A grenade!" Bluff exclaimed. "What will it do?"

"Who knows!" Haven shouted. "Use it!"

Akimu pulled the pin and threw it toward the charging Xynd. The grenade ignited and spewed out smoke, filling the area with a thick veil. For the charging Xynd, the air became hazy, and their visibility blurred. Some of them shouted in panic, their eyes dripping with tears from the grenade's gas.

"Smoke? That's all it does?" Bluff shouted.

"It'll give us time!" Haven responded.

The Xynd hesitated and slowed their charging. More of them covered their eyes, blinded by the smoke. They stepped back out of fear. But plenty still shot their arrows.

Epoch, fierce with determination, threw Ruddy across the divide, and he landed next to Lunar. It was Sven's turn, but the

Giant's success shattered as an arrow, sharp as demise's decree, found its mark on his shoulder. Though being a powerful behemoth, he screamed in pain. A guttural roar echoed through the cave.

Akimu stood up and shielded Epoch's upper body. Bluff hustled over with his shield to protect Epoch's lower half. Charged with the primal struggle of survival, Epoch threw Sven across the chasm, who landed harshly, barely reaching the other side. Lunar lifted him from the edge, dragging him behind a large rock.

Blood ran down Epoch's shoulder, chest, and arm. The arrow certainly did damage. He staggered; his resolve remained unbroken. He threw Akimu and Bluff across the divide; his teeth clenched against searing agony. He turned to face the unseen foes lurking in the shadows and smoke. He stumbled over to Haven.

Haven wrapped a rope around Epoch's waist and tied it. Then he tied the other end around himself. "Throw me across. When I'm there, the others will grab hold of me. Do your best to jump across. If you don't make it, the rest of us will pull you up," Haven shouted.

Epoch nodded. "Got it."

From the other side of the chasm, Ruddy continued to sling pellets at the relentless natives. Akimu, Sven, and Lunar grabbed stones from the cave floor, each a weapon honed by the ancient cave's hand. Their eyes locked on their adversaries, who hid in the smoke. In unison, the three launched their stones. They found their marks, striking against flesh and bone. The natives reacted with surprise and fury. It gave Haven and Epoch just enough time to execute their escape.

Haven threw his shield across the chasm. Then Epoch threw him, but just as Haven made it to the other side, another arrow pierced Epoch, this time into his back. He screamed in agony.

The Xynd walked through the barrier of smoke, closing their eyes as they did so.

"Jump!" the Assemblage shouted as they all grabbed onto Haven. Epoch sprinted toward the chasm. He jumped as far as he could but landed just short. He fell into the hole, which yanked Haven toward it. The six were now in a tug-of-war match with Epoch's dangling body. The six pulled with all their strength. Their heels dug into the ground, and they gained traction.

The natives stood at the chasm's edge, firing every arrow they had. "Hubah! Zu! Hubah! Zu!"

"Oh, shut up!" Ruddy yelled. He shot a series of pellets in their direction, hitting two of them in the face.

Epoch grabbed onto the cliff's edge. His friends held onto him and pulled him up. A third arrow pierced into Epoch's back before they pulled him up to safety.

Ruddy shot more pellets. Lunar threw rocks. One of which actually hit a native.

The onslaught of arrows and needles continued. An arrow pierced into Bluff's erokan. The force knocked his head back to the ground.

"Bluff!" Haven exclaimed. Anxiously, Haven checked Bluff's head and saw where the arrow stuck. But the circlet prevented the arrow from piercing his head.

The Xynd were relentless and determined. Several of them pushed a long piece of wood across the divide—it was, in fact, a bridge. Their chant changed: "Kee nee! Kee nee! Bah!"

"They have a bridge!" Ruddy shouted to the others.

"Who carries a bridge around?" Lunar shrieked.

Akimu acted quickly. As the arrows momentarily ceased, he pulled a grenade out of the bag of tricks. This one was red. Akimu looked at it, uncertain of what the color difference meant. It didn't matter, though.

"Just throw it," Haven advised, desperate for a solution to their predicament. Akimu pulled the pin and tossed it at the bridge. As the first native made it across, the grenade exploded. The blast sent a shockwave in all directions. The explosion shattered part of the cave's roof above the chasm. A crash of tumbling rocks collided, shaking the ground.

After the dust settled, they saw the damage. The cave had collapsed enough to create a wall of rocky debris in front of the chasm, destroying the bridge. They were safe.

"That should stop their arrows," Sven sighed.

"So the red grenades explode," Haven said. Akimu nodded, his eyebrows raised—a sincere expression from a usually stolid person.

Bluff sat up; the arrow still pierced his erokan. He shook his head, a little unclear about what had happened. "Did we get 'em?" he asked.

"Thanks to Akimu, yes. We got them," Haven replied.

They took a moment to treat their wounds, especially those of Epochs. Once Bluff collected himself, he went to work on Epoch, who sat silently, his immense form dwarfing Bluffs. A flicker of gratitude glimmered in Epoch's eyes, watching Bluff's quiet care for him in the cold cave.

The rest of them had scratches and bruises. They counted themselves blessed as they all pulled arrows and needles from their shields and armor.

Instead of staying in one place, they moved forward despite injuries. The cave proved long and dark. Lunar's skin lit up the jagged path ahead. They had no lanterns to light their way, so they thanked Lunar in different ways that befit their personalities. The magnificent blue fluorescent walls were far behind them now. Just bleak, dark coldness ahead. But onward, they went.

They traveled some distance, cracking jokes and telling stories. Despite quickly getting on each other's nerves, Lunar and Sven shared a similar sense of humor, which all the others found endearing. Several times, they asked Haven what the next move was, but he did not know the way. He said, "Onward." Again, doubts filled his heart.

The cave's roof gradually lowered, plus the cave floor slanted upward. It became so narrow that they were all crouching, making climbing difficult. To their frustration, they eventually found themselves before a cave-in.

"A dead end?" Sven said, exhausted.

They all sat there, discouraged. Tired, Epoch rested on the dirt. Bluff gave him water.

Sven looked around at their desperate situation. "Trapped between two cave-ins," he said cynically. He drank from his water canteen, looking over to Akimu, who sat quietly. "How do you travel this far without water?" he asked.

Akimu reached inside his cloak with a deft hand. He pulled out a canteen, its contours barely distinguishable, shimmering faintly from Lunar's silver light. Raising it to his lips, he took a silent sip, his expression unchanging as he savored the drink.

"You secretive shadow," Sven replied. "What else do you hide from us?" Akimu shook his finger, then raised it to his lips. Sven smirked, admiring the Flame Shadow's covert methods.

"I want one of those," Lunar said, watching Akimu take another sip.

Sitting there among Lunar's glow, each shared their frustrations. But Haven responded constructively. He saw a faint light coming from the cave wall across from him. To better inspect it, he needed the surroundings darker. "Lunar, cover yourself," he insisted as he moved toward the soft ray of light. Sven was quick to toss a blanket over Lunar.

"What is that?" Haven whispered. He crawled on all fours toward it. The others took notice and wondered the same.

"What is what?" Lunar asked from under the blanket.

Haven touched the tiny glimmer of light while the others watched him. He pushed his hand against the rock. It moved slightly, showing emptiness behind it. He pushed harder, and it fell backward, crumbling into pieces. After removing some other stones, much of the wall collapsed. It was, in fact, an opening into another cave.

All of them, besides Lunar, who still sat clueless under the blanket, joined Haven at the cave entrance. Inside, it was bright, and a dreamy fog filled the air. Through it, they could see what appeared to be an angelic woman standing up on a pedestal. Below her were two other women, much smaller.

Peering into the haze, Haven wondered out loud. "What is this place?"

~~~

They crawled into the dreamy fog. The roof in this cave was much higher by at least twenty feet. They each stood up and looked around. Upon closer inspection, they were looking upon some shrine—the Traitress Shrine, to be exact. It comprised three stone statues endearing holy women. White flowers decorated the area.

Rubble, too, surrounded the shrine. They gazed upwards, eyes widening at seeing a gaping hole in the cave's roof, a portal to the outside world. At some point, a portion of the cave's roof collapsed. Sunlight streamed in, illuminating their surroundings.

Each young man inspected the area with interest. Ruddy, however, looked with suspicion. Akimu, too, tensed up. Bluff noticed their concern and questioned them about it.

Ruddy looked at Akimu with despair. "Did we stumble on something we shouldn't of?"

"Why? What is it?" Haven asked.

"Do you remember the Age of Treachery?" Ruddy asked, inspecting the white flowers.

Haven thought momentarily and recalled learning a thing or two years ago while studying at the Great Library. "Yes. Something about an insurgence led by women?"

"More like mass murder," Ruddy replied. This was enough to get everyone's attention, and all six listened to him intently.

He recalled all he knew about this age of treason—a tragic time in Wunduria's long history. Ruddy slowly turned around to face his comrades. And so this dark piece of history was told:

"There was a rebellion by certain women who devised a plan against what they perceived to be men's cruel dominance over them. A certain segment of these so-called 'enlightened' women segregated themselves from every kingdom. They all hid in caves, calling themselves Mother Earth. They plotted to destroy man's power over them. They brew potions and elixirs. They forsook their oath as healers and created a deadly plague instead."

The other six listened intently; Akimu lowered his head, ashamed at this part of history. He knew this unfortunate truth already.

Ruddy continued, almost whispering, "Certain men joined their duplicity, eunuchs who acted as servants. Eventually, their combined treachery weaponized an elegant White Spurn flower with a sweet fragrance. The flower induced sleep in all those who smelled it. But it was most effective for men. In their slumber, men would perish, never waking again. Mother Earth planted the flowers throughout the land for their twisted view of virtue and balance. It spread like weeds."

Haven looked over at the white flowers that surrounded them. His eyes darted from one end of the cave to the other. His voice wavered. "I remember. The scent killed hundreds on the first day. Their agenda to kill men succeeded. Husbands, fathers, and sons all fell victim. Within a month, over five thousand fell to its poison. It took a crusade of women to fight Mother Earth and to eradicate the white spurn flower. The Mother Crusaders of Wunduria found victory."

Ruddy nodded, then concluded all he knew, "They called the white flower of death the Widow Maker. In the end, over ten thousand men perished."

The others looked at each other, worried they might have wandered into the wrong place. "These can't be the flowers," Sven gasped. "My father told me this tale long ago. He said the flower no longer existed. The last of them were abandoned inside a dry, dark place to wither away and die."

Ruddy and Akimu understood the tale the same way. "Maybe this is that dark place. Only the roof fell in and gave it life," Ruddy proposed.

"Let's not get ahead of ourselves," Haven cautioned. "This cave is dry. Life needs water."

Bluff stepped forward. "Then how do the flowers grow if there is no water?"

Lunar sat down, yawning. "I don't have the energy to believe such a thing. Sounds made up."

"But it's not," Ruddy replied. But he, too, sat down yawning.

"Would you two shut up and get over here!" Haven yelled, inspecting the hole in the roof above. "Lunar, give me your rope. We'll climb our way out of here." But Lunar did not respond to his request. "Lunar!" he shouted. Haven looked over at his friends, who were all on the ground, either yawning or asleep.

"No, no, no!" he shouted. "Get up!"

That's when he heard a giant collision and shattering of rocks. He looked behind him to find an opening in the cave leading to the outside. Epoch grabbed his wrapped, injured shoulder, wincing with pain. Despite his injury, he had punched a hole into the rocky wall. "I made a way out," he muttered before falling to the ground, exhausted.

"Let's grab them and get out of here," Haven insisted, but he found Epoch on the ground, asleep. He realized he hadn't much time. He dragged each one out of the cave with every bit of energy left in him. Soon, they all lay outside the cave on a precipice that overlooked the green flourishing fields below. Haven was the only one left standing. But tiredness took hold of him, too. Struggling to stand, he looked outward into the sky and saw a remarkable sight. High above, floating like a dream and promise, was a skyship.

This was no ordinary skyship. It was one with giant sails, like an old seaworthy vessel. The sails were full of wind, and it flew toward them speedily. Behind it was the beauty of dusk. An orange blaze of color painted the horizon. The sky spoke of peace as Haven's eyes drooped and blinked slowly. His eyes rested. He reached toward the skyship, but, overcome by tiredness, he dropped to the ground. And he was asleep.

12

SHINE MARINER

Night lurked above the clouds. Dark pushed the warm sun down, and an aura of pink lifted from the horizon into the heavens and disappeared somewhere beyond that. The young men were all safe on the deck of the mighty skyship. Their rescue came from Jehu's brother Shumi, and they all woke up on his flying vessel.

His majestic ship glided through the skies, soaring above the earthly constraints that bound mere mortals. The surrounding skyscape was a canvas of shifting colors. The setting sun painted it with crimson, gold, and amethyst. Only the cloud vapors and crisp airs accompanied them at these heights.

Six of the seven sat with their backs against the taffrail on the open deck. Each with an empty bowl next to them. They were quick to consume the soup provided.

Shumi was at the helm, piloting the ship carried by the evening winds. His daughter, Emmy, attended to the needs of the seven young men and helped them regain their coherency and health. Though her father told her not to feed them, she did anyway. "Mother would have fed them," she argued.

Emmy's beauty matched the sunset sky, ablaze with warmth and joy. As she brought a cup of spicy Stir Soup to Haven, the other six, weary and weak, gazed at her smile. She was easy on the eyes, especially with all they had seen in the past two days.

Still resting on a cot, Haven heard the sails flap above. He felt the breeze on his skin. He awoke to the calming sound. Emmy put her soft hand on his. He opened his eyes slowly to find her smiling. She was a beautiful girl, probably his age, with blonde hair that rested gently on her shoulders. Her eyes, the color of amber, were sweet and easy to look into. Such a pretty face to see after fearing death.

His thoughts rushed back to him, and he sat up, worried. He wondered where exactly he was. His expression was clear to her.

She handed him the bowl of soup. "Please, stay calm. You and your friends are safe. Eat this. It will help with the headache."

He accepted the bowl and sipped from it, which soothed his aching head. "Where are we?"

"My father's ship. My uncle asked us to carry you across the Hemlock Yards."

"What about the flowers? We found the widow maker..." he said to her, concerned.

"No." She smiled. "Those were not widow makers. Just an earlier concoction. You're safe."

"Concoction?" he replied with a raised eyebrow.

"Yes, one of the earliest versions," she explained. "Those wicked women of old created many terrible things. You'll have a headache, that's all."

Haven sighed in relief. "Thank you," he whispered. She smiled with the grace of a dear friend and held his hand. "You'll feel much better soon. By midnight, we'll reach the north side barrier. My father has a place for you to sleep and regain your strength."

"Thank you," he responded, comforted by her caring nature. She saw Haven to be handsome. He returned her gentle touch by intertwining his fingers with hers. For a moment, they locked eyes, and their youthful hearts explored the fleeting nuances of flirtation. For Haven, her softness was a reward. For Emmy, it meant much more. She leaned in to kiss him, but her father would have none of that.

He called out her name angrily. "Emmy! Get over here!" She responded abruptly and left Haven's side.

Lunar sat beside Haven's cot. "She's pretty. I think she likes you," he said, nudging Haven's side.

Haven blushed and looked back up at the sails. *What a wonderful place to be.* "To live among the clouds," he said. "Heavenly, isn't it?"

Lunar agreed and explained that he expressed gratitude to the pilot and Emmy. Shumi, however, hadn't much to say to any of them. Shumi was nothing like his brother, Jehu. Instead, he was a grumpy old man without manners. Emmy, however, was the polite one, decent and sweet.

After finishing the soup, Haven walked across the main deck and leaned against the ship's ledge. He looked down at the ground far below and then up at the pink horizon. Such peace and warmth—a fine reward after what they had gone through in the caves.

The sun dipped behind the horizon. One by one, the six exchanged glances with Haven, their eyes filled with gratitude. Their nods and subtle smiles spoke volumes, silently acknowledging his bravery and leadership.

They joined him to admire the tranquil moment. Amid his comrades, Sven felt a sense of honor. "After we kill Snarlag, all will know our story. My father will value me like he does my older brothers."

Epoch rotated his aching shoulder before patting Sven's back. "I value you, Sven." He said.

"Thanks, big guy," Sven replied, smiling.

"What is your hope?" Bluff asked Haven.

After a quiet thought, he replied, "I want to lead you to the summit and finish our task. If we somehow survive, I want us to return home and see the lives of those we saved."

Moved by Haven's words, his friends rejoiced in their hearts and nodded. "That is a good thing," Bluff commented. "I'll follow you to the end."

The others all agreed. "I'll follow you too."

Together, they watched the stars emerge like scattered jewels. The twinkling lights guided the skyship's path through the purple clouds. And as the sun dipped below the horizon, casting its farewell, Haven's heart returned to the memory of his father. He felt the pendant that hung from his neck. *I wish he could see me now.*

Inspired by the billowing sails and fading light of day, Sven sang his Norseman psalm:

We sail till the end
Valor and pride's intent
A Viking's back to the wind
A Viking's back to the wind
Never give in

~ ~ ~

They reached the north side barrier. North of it, rugged terrain lay ahead: a bog, a wasteland, and then the Blind Mountains. They all felt intimidated by its potential dangers.

Shumi docked his skyship on a wooden dry dock just outside his little stone house. "Get off my ship!" He yelled repeatedly. After getting off, they tried to introduce themselves, but each received a scowl.

After they stepped onto Shumi's land, he spoke quickly and curtly, "The only reason I am helping you this day is my dear brother requested I do so. I am sure he deserted you to run off on one of his wild escapades. This is as far north as I will fly you. The winds north of here are dangerous, as is that mountain mist. You may sleep in my barn tonight if you choose. It's cold at night, but my cattle do just fine. I expect you to be gone by morning. If you're not, there will be trouble."

Before Shumi walked away, he gave a fair warning: "Keep your eyes and hands off my daughter, or you'll leave here eyeless and handless." He took one step forward and then stopped. "Oh, a Feral Girl lives in the woods behind my home. She is precious to my Emmy. Keep your squirmy hands off her, too." He then grabbed Emmy's hand and pulled her toward their home.

"Nice to meet you all!" she politely shouted.

The mentioned Feral Girl caught Ruddy's attention. He followed Shumi and asked about the girl. Haven, however, pulled him back. "Never mind her, Ruddy."

Shumi, a retired pilot living by the north barrier, moved quickly for an old man across his grassy corral. His glorious skyship was a memento that reminded him of a better youth—a time he wasn't so bitter.

Haven glanced back at the skyship. On one side of the craft, in big white letters, was its name, *Shine Mariner*. *What does that mean?*

As the seven approached the barn, Ruddy noticed a young girl, perhaps his age, running out from the woods behind Shumi's house. The moon gave just enough light for him to see her. She skipped through a field and paused when she saw him. Her heart filled with excitement. She looked at him curiously. They met eyes, both caught up in wonder.

The young girl was very short. She wore what seemed to be a pilot cap, but with ears sticking out from the top—ears like that of a cat. Pink flowers hung below each ear. Her long, curly dark hair appeared clean and kept, which was a surprise for someone who lived in the wild. Ruddy was most impressed by her delicate, beautiful face decorated with freckles. Ruddy's entire world stopped as he looked at her.

Haven noticed Ruddy's distraction. "Keep your eyes forward," he instructed, trying to keep Ruddy from trouble.

She allowed herself one final peek at Ruddy. She then turned and ran away. Graceful like a young gazelle. Innocent as a hind.

"She has my heart," Ruddy said as Haven pulled him toward the barn.

"I'm sorry, my red friend. But she is none of your business. Maybe after we save the island from destruction."

"Maybe." Ruddy smiled, blushing and redder than usual.

Disappointed, Ruddy complied, but not without complaint. She didn't leave his mind, though. No one had any hold over that. He would even dream of her later that night. Sleep allowed his heart freedom to explore this new love of his.

The Assemblage nestled into the barn hesitantly due to what else slept there. Shumi's cattle comprised Greyt Bulls and Greyt Cows. Known for their aggressive nature, these animals were rare on the island, primarily because of how difficult and dangerous they were to handle. "They look dangerous," Lunar whispered.

Sven replied, "They are. Only a mighty man can farm them."

To which Lunar whispered, "I don't take that old grump to be mighty."

"Then he must be a brave man," Sven countered. "We have a few of these giant beasts outside our village. The cows will follow once you earn a Greyt Bull's trust and loyalty. If the old man can push a Greyt around, he can push us too—even Epoch. Believe me. Shumi must be mighty and brave."

"Why have them, though?" Lunar asked.

Sven smiled, eager to answer. "A glass of Greyt milk can sustain a man for a month. Not to mention that these animals provide excellent protection. Who knows the lawless bandits that roam this bleak land?"

"Let's sleep," Haven interrupted. "We have a long way to go tomorrow."

The six of them complied, all exhausted.

Despite their fear of the cattle, they fell asleep quickly. The Greyt Cows snored loudly, but the sounds were soothing to the ears. It was not like the snoring one would hear from fat men. It was more of a low, consistent purr, incredibly deep. It healed their aching bodies.

Before falling asleep, Haven thought of his leisure afternoons with Thunder and the sheep he once watched over. He missed shepherding them and hearing their little noises.

His mother then came to mind. He hoped her holiday was one of relaxation and that she was happy. He imagined her busy with joyful things. Then he was asleep.

13

OTHER TROUBLES

Jehu's troubles were considerably different. Amidst the emerald hills, the revered Geezer rode astride his magnificent steed, its ebony mane billowing in the wind like a silken banner of determination. His weathered cloak trailed behind him as they galloped toward the towering Castle of Hills.

His eyes were alive with ancient wisdom, foreseeing challenges of terrible things in the castle's looming silhouette. The moon painted the sky behind it with supreme shades of blue. With every stride of his horse, the rhythmic pounding of hooves brought further worry to his heart.

Appropriately named, the castle stood on top of what some might mistake as a mountain. The fortress rested on a series of hills, one larger than the next. The ground was lush, with ongoing green uplands and trees—a land full of life.

Exhausted by the travel, Jehu's horse was ready to give out. But he had to keep it moving. Time was not his ally. The crow, which had brought him the red ribbon of peril, flew overhead, accompanying his travel.

He rode up and down the Paleland drumlins and reached the castle far quicker than anyone would believe. His horse rode fast, heeding his every command to sprint relentlessly. But it exhausted itself nearly to death. As soon as Jehu dismounted it, a servant to the king cared for the horse. "Revive it, nurture it!" Jehu shouted to the servant.

The red marker on the crow's foot was a sign of fatality. Jehu needed to speak with the King of the Paleland Kingdom. King

Aidan Redd required his attention, which Jehu knew not to be a good thing.

Upon arrival, Jehu found the castle on lockdown. Fewer than the ordinary number of guards were at their posts. Something grim was at hand. He dismounted his famished horse and ran toward the castle gate. A single guard led him to the throne room. But when he entered, he found the throne empty. A courtier was there, kneeling beside the throne, weeping. Jehu approached him.

"Where is the king?" he demanded, face white with fear.

The courtier sniveled and looked up at him with tearful eyes. He stammered something incomprehensible. Jehu shook the man. "Where?"

"Jehu," a hushed voice called behind him near a passageway. Jehu turned to find Lief, the king's nephew. Jehu feared the worst.

Lief led him to the king, explaining this and that of a tremendous setback, a great tragedy. They soon entered the king's dining hall. There, alone at a table, slumped in his chair, King Aidan Redd sat behind a plate of food. The scent of which was excellent and pleasing.

"Jehu," the king muttered with a cough. Jehu rushed over to sit beside him at the table. He gasped, looking over the king's broken body.

Unable to sit up, the king winced in the thick of his suffering. He bit into a piece of meat and then dropped it back onto the plate. He chewed sloppily. Juices dripped from his chin. With Jehu's help, he took a sip from his goblet—a feat he struggled to achieve. Jehu teared up. "Aidan, what has happened?"

"She destroyed us," he replied, unable to lift his head. Each word he forced through his lips. "She's too quick." He winced, lifting blood-soaked rags from his now useless knees. His legs needed amputation. Blood puddled below his chair.

"Tell me what you know," Jehu said, his voice choked.

The king nodded, trying to sit up, bellowing an awful cry. "Snarlag," he panted. "I sent two battalions up the mountainside. We found one last path to the summit...the last of our soldiers. We climbed, sure of our ascent. But her ropes intercepted us. She wills them as she pleases, swatting us like flies," the king panted again, angry this time.

Jehu leaned in to hear him better. The king's eyes had glossed over. "Jehu...I sent for you because you need to know this..." he whispered, prepared to meet death. "She spoke to me."

Jehu's expression changed from concern to dread. "Snarlag?" Jehu whispered. "How can this be?"

"It spoke using the mouth of my son. She pierced a root into Patrick. He hung there like a puppet. His voice, her words." He wept, struggling to finish.

Jehu pleaded with him, "Aidan, son of Oisin. Find your strength, I beg you. What did she say?"

"She knows we're coming for her. She knows our every plan. She told me," he muttered.

Horror consumed Jehu. His hands shook with worry. His eyes teared up.

Aidan Redd, the once mighty king, dropped his head in defeat. With his final breath, he spoke once more, "Bron. Bron knows." Then, a blank stare filled King Aidan Redd's eyes. He died that very moment.

Jehu wept. He then closed Aidan's eyes with his hand and whispered a dirge.

Believing to hear the king correctly, Jehu thought of his last words. "Bron knows." He stood up, puzzled by the mention of the king's chief military advisor.

Entering the room wearing her black caftan and golden shawl, the queen saw the Geezer beside her dead husband. She had cut her hair in despair, having nothing to hide her face full of tears.

With great respect, Jehu kneeled before her. "Queen Ialdya, my deepest condolences."

She was a woman worthy of honor. As queen, she helped unite her people through unrest. The Paleland population, from small to great, held her in high esteem, as did those from other kingdoms.

Ialdya looked down at her friend with teary eyes. "Please stand, Jehu," she said softly. He stood and hugged her like a father would a daughter. "I must speak with you in secret."

Jehu nodded at her request. They entered a quiet chamber. There, she spoke in whispers. "My husband condemned one man to an insufferable death. Before he left for the battle, he cursed Bron Crowl many times. The man is corrupt beyond imagination. He and Aidan argued at great lengths."

"Argued?" Jehu whispered through his gray mustache.

She explained, eager for Jehu's ageless wisdom to fix all things. "You must know Bron conspires with the rockworm. He values its power. And he speaks of many horrible things to come." She grabbed hold of Jehu's arms tightly. "I heard him speak of a coming plague."

"A plague when we are nearing destruction? I must speak with Bron immediately," he insisted.

"Aidan shut him up in his room. Jehu, you must discover his deceit."

"I will, Ialdya."

She straightened her shoulders. "My people will have a strong queen as their leader, but I must follow what is right. I must first mourn my husband's passing."

Jehu agreed and thanked the virtuous queen. He then fled to seek the contemptuous Bron Crowl, whose chamber was quite far from all the other rooms, down many corridors and halls, away from all those decent and fair. As Jehu rushed to find it, he recalled how Bron was a loathsomely deceitful man—a politician full of avarice inclinations. Jehu had warned Aidan not to make Bron the head military advisor. However, Geezer's advice is only helpful when adhered to.

~ ~ ~

Upon arriving at Bron's room, Jehu found a castle guard lying dead outside it. Jehu dared to enter anyway. The heavy wooden door creaked as he stepped inside the dimly lit chamber, his cloak trailing behind him like wisps of smoke as the dust rose. An aura hung heavy with an eerie silence, broken only by the soft shuffle of his measured steps. In a shadowed corner, sitting stiffly in a chair, someone sat alone in the dark.

Bron held a piercing gaze on the newcomer, lifting a crooked smile on his thin lips. Although evil existed there, Jehu's presence exuded a calming goodness, contrasting with the ominous atmosphere of Bron's chamber.

Bron's complexion bore the markings of a soul steeped in gloominess: pallid skin stretched taut over sharp angles. His stare held a glint of malice, and his thin, chiseled lips twisted into a mocking smirk, revealing yellow teeth.

With a voice as chilling as the room, he taunted Jehu, aiming to unsettle his unwavering composure. "Strange for a sage to disturb me at this hour. What brings you here, Geezer?" he questioned, his voice dripping with disdain and arrogance. His voice was much lower than usual, which kept Jehu keenly observant, his eyes scanning the chamber with practiced precision. Despite Bron's attempt to provoke, Jehu stood stoically, with a quiet confidence that irked Bron further.

"Bron Crowl, son of Jadus, what hides in your thoughts?" sensible Jehu asked with a fixed glare on the man. Bron's nefarious intentions hung heavy. His smirk widened, his teeth dripping with drool.

The conversation unfolded, and Jehu's suspicion deepened, sensing the tendrils of malice in Bron's every word and gesture. The man's appearance revealed an unnatural and still manner, almost as if the life force within him had dimmed. His complexion was pale, his features rigid. Jehu surmised the darkness Bron harbored within had now entirely consumed him, rendering him an almost puppet figure in the dimly lit room.

As Bron spoke empty speech, a flicker of movement caught Jehu's attention, a subtle shift in the chamber's stone wall behind Bron's chair. He spotted a reckless crack. Its jagged line snaking upwards within the shadows. His sight lingered on the rift, a furrow appearing between his brow as he pondered its significance. Unwilling to reveal his discovery, Jehu maintained his composed facade. He thought this crack might hold secrets beyond what met the eye—a telling of something hidden, something crucial that would explain Bron's unusualness.

The twisted Bron rose from his seat. He lifted as if he were a puppet on strings. Something controlled his movements. It was, in fact, one of Snarlag's appendages. It worked Bron like a figurine, entering through the wall and slithering inside his spine. He was under the enemy's control. Jehu's eyes widened, and his body dripped in a cold sweat.

Bron's voice, tinged with a bitter edge, sliced through the emptiness between him and the Geezer. "I have lost myself in this madness. What began as an attempt to safeguard my ambitions has condemned us all," the true Bron spoke.

"What have you done?" Jehu asked, stepping back.

Bron whimpered a haunting admission of greed. "I have betrayed my people." His sniveling words carried undeniable guilt. "I betrayed the king. Snarlag knows my every thought, my every secret. Our every secret. The house of Redd will fall."

Jehu lifted his staff before himself. "You selfish pawn," Jehu growled.

"I know," Bron cried, his eyes rimmed with tears. "I told her everything. She knows of our ascent upon her, including the seven you've sent out. She has seduced every kingdom and has her grip on many minds." His body twitched under Snarlag's control. He jerked his head, trying to keep his coherency. "Those under her control have betrayed Wunduria. I can hear them sharing secrets, Jehu. I can hear their thoughts; I can hear hers. She knows we aim to destroy her."

Her appendage lifted him, pushing him forward. His feet dragged along the floor. Her root stuck into his back, directing him at Jehu. Bron no longer had the will to fight her off. He dangled in the air, and his voice lowered to a deep snarl. It was Snarlag's words now.

"You will not stop me, old man. I will destroy everything," she threatened.

"We will fight you to our bitter deaths, you harlot," Jehu responded, angered by her courtships with all the kingdom's betrayers.

"I have pierced the hearts and minds of many advisors. I know of every plan to stop me," she snarled.

Indulged in her practices of mixing her ropes into flesh, she pushed Bron further into her control. "Man will not destroy me. I will crumble this land into the seas. I hold it together; without me, all life will rot, wither and die. A plague will befall you."

Jehu stepped back toward the doorway. Several other roots penetrated the wall, pushing Bron's chair to the floor.

With his last morsel of energy, he gained control over his speech and cried out. "Run, Jehu! Run from my guilt! Escape!"

That is precisely what Jehu did. He ran toward the door and fled the horror. She laughed maniacally through her human voice box as Jehu darted toward the castle's exit. "I am your king now! Bow to me!" she screamed.

Jehu escaped but found his horse still exhausted from their arduous journey. It was then that he caught sight of a beautiful thing. Out toward the east, coming down through the clouds, a glorious skyship sailed among the stars in the wind with its sails full of gust.

With his old eyes, he spotted the Buccaneer flag raised and flapping in the moonlight. He pulled a flare out of his bag and lit it. It ascended into the sky as a beacon.

He shouted to the skyship as if his voice would carry that far into the night. As the vessel approached overhead, a rope dropped from its side. It lowered from its heights just above the castle of hills. Jehu grabbed hold of it. He readied himself to hold on tight. "Time to fly," he said nervously.

He ascended gracefully toward the magnificent flying ship. His long, silvered hair billowed in the wind, and his eyes shimmered with ancient wisdom. He clung to the sturdy rope. Despite its fibers' harsh feel against his old hands, Jehu held on tightly, eyeing the craft far above him. The ship, adorned with tattered sails and gleaming brass, soared through the clouds, its crew of daring Buccaneers cheering as they hauled him aboard.

As he set his feet on deck, the creaking timbers and Buccaneer's cheers brought an air of unlikely composure in this improbable meeting in the sky. He thanked those who pulled him up from the misfortune he experienced far below. Suddenly, Gamba Tru's sister, Glori, the vessel's captain, stood before him.

There she stood with an aura of unyielding strength, a tempest incarnate full of life in the cold air of the skies. Clad in weather-beaten leather adorned with intricate golden trinkets, her attire boasted the tales of countless conquests. Strands of raven-black hair cascaded over her shoulders, framing a face of fierce determination. Tattoos adorned her arms and hands, inked in vibrant hues.

"Good of you to join us, Jehu," she remarked.

"Thank you, Glori. But I bring dreadful news," he replied, short of breath. "I hope your armada is prepared for the worst. The enemy is prepared to fight us."

She nodded as if she already knew what he alluded to. "We already know. Snarlag's arms have destroyed most of our ships and island homes. Our leaders have conspired with her. They have betrayed us."

"She attacked your islands?" Jehu asked, alertness in his eyes as he straightened his crooked glasses.

"Yes. Snarlag's arms lifted from the seas that surrounded our ship's harbor. She sank many ships, even pulling some from the skies above," she explained, leading Jehu toward a map of Wunduria. She pointed at the islands of Tortuga Nue. "The worm laid our towns in ruins. We escaped with only a few ships."

"It gets worse," Jehu panted. "Snarlag has rooted herself deep into the minds of key figures throughout the land. Tapping into their knowledge, she knows we are coming for her. I am afraid that she knows more than we can afford. I just encountered Bron Crowl, one of her puppets."

Emerging from a private cabin behind the map, Gamba Tru bustled out. His swagger was unmistaken as he strolled toward them. "Crowl is a serpent, always has been," he said, confident in his speech. "If Snarlag can tap into people's minds, that would explain the rising evil powers that ousted me as king."

Excited to see him, Jehu grabbed Gamba's forearm firmly.

"Your presence is much needed," Jehu chimed.

Gamba pointed to the map, revealing the course of their other skyships. "We must meet back with what's left of the armada before they reach the mountains. The winds will act as a swirling shield, preventing passage to the summit."

"I know a trick that will carry us through," Glori replied. "Besides, we have no choice but to fight the winds there,"

"Snarlag will be ready for us," Jehu claimed.

"Then we will fall on her when she least suspects it," Glori stated, staring into the skies before them.

"We will reign down punishment," Gamba said confidently. "We will have our revenge."

14

BOG AND MISFORTUNE

Shumi opened the barn doors and woke his giant Greyt beasts. The Assemblage awoke to the sound of the cattle moving about. Shumi shouted commands and prodded many of them with a steel rod.

Haven led his comrades out of the barn. They found Emmy preparing glasses filled with Greyt Cow's milk outside of it. It was a hearty breakfast for anyone who dared drink it. Six of the seven drank, even though the milk was bitter and difficult to keep in their bellies. Lunar, who spit his first sip out, declined to drink anymore. Emmy giggled as Sven finished every drop of Lunar's glass. They thanked her kindly.

She handed them long black coats designed for the harsh, swampy environment as they departed. "These will keep you dry," she said softly.

She also handed Haven a mint candy, hoping he'd enjoy it. He thanked her before popping it into his mouth as he put on the coat. She wanted to see him another day. He felt the same. Their mutual blushful glances told each other so. He kissed her cheek before leaving.

The sweeter surprise was for Ruddy. His new crush, the young Feral Girl, sprinted toward him. They met behind the barn, out of Shumi's sight. He looked at her, holding her hands. "Since I saw you last night under the stars, I cannot get you out of my mind," he said. She smiled and kissed his cheek.

"My name is Kidty," she said quietly with a sweet feminine pitch. Ruddy found it undeniably cute. He smiled, and then they both snickered.

He could barely make a reply but found the strength to. "People call me Ruddy, but my parents named me Deklin."

She whispered his name back to him. *Deklin.*

They looked into each other's eyes. Hers were brown; his were green. With her tiny and gentle hands, she felt the red marking on his face, painted fresh the day before. "What are they?" she asked.

"They mark me as one united with the creatures of this land."

"Lovely," she said softly.

Desperate for his companionship, she looked beyond him at the others, who were now far ahead of him, heading toward the bog. She stared back into his eyes. "Will you return to me?"

Death at the summit meant little to him now. "Nothing will stop me from seeing you again," he said, smiling.

"I will wait for you every day," she said, then pressed her lips onto his. Before he could embrace it, she darted off into the field. He instantly ached without her touch. As she disappeared, he drifted into feelings of affection.

After a bit of lollygagging, he caught up with his friends. Haven asked where he had been, but Ruddy was too infatuated to speak.

Haven saw him aglow with blushing affection. His comrade had an even greater reason to save the island—love.

As they marched forward, dragonflies followed behind Deklin. They encircled him, buzzing an exciting tune. The entire Assemblage heard cardinals singing above them in the trees. Deklin then whistled with their song. It was an enjoyable inspiration and a blissful start to the day's journey.

All seven pointed their heads north and moved in a line. Almost soldier-like. Haven made it to the front and led the way. The Kremin's Bog, with all its mud, was ahead of them. "To the unknown, boys!" He shouted.

~ ~ ~

The bog was what one would think it to be. The seven slogged through the wet ground, moving slowly, knee-deep, into the mire. Their heavy boots, coated in sludge, made each step difficult. They each complained at the start.

Lunar, however, continued to be vocal about his soggy plight. Sven—bothered by the number of mosquitos—couldn't stand the Pulveran's whining any longer. It drove him to a breaking point.

Sven turned around and pushed Lunar into the dank marsh. The albino fell into the smelly water like a stone. The others had a good laugh. But Lunar rose from the slime, angered and ready to fight. He swung at Sven, who was quick to dodge the swing. He even laughed. Sven welcomed the tussle and called Lunar many objectionable things. Insulted, Lunar threw a handful of mud into Sven's face. They sought to brawl before Haven could settle things. He tore them apart and told the Pulveran he had it coming and to stop complaining. He demanded Sven control his anger.

"Quit your quarrel!" He ordered. "I know tensions are high, but stay focused. Do not fear trudging through the mire. Fear standing still."

BOG AND MISFORTUNE

As they journeyed, a sense of camaraderie blossomed. They shared songs and laughter, and even the strange noises of the bog's reptilian life couldn't dampen their spirits. The unique habitat of Kremin's Bog was a treasure trove of unusual living things, and they were all in it together.

Ruddy collected certain plants into jars, as he had been doing wherever he went. He also saw tiny creatures the others paid no mind to. He hoped to see a Frotle. These unique little frogs had turtle-like shells on their backs.

Ruddy carried one with him for a bit as they trudged their way through the spongy ground. It mostly sat on his shoulder until it hopped off into some shrubs. The little thing made a silly sound. It was a croak but ended with a slight hiccup sound. It was funny to hear. Lunar made a sound very similar to it, causing Sven to laugh. All seven took turns imitating the sound. Eventually, they fell into a laughing fit when the Giant tried.

Epoch's attempt to mimic the sound fell hilariously short. He could only make a bumbling noise. They laughed a good while, much to his dislike. "Laugh all you want, little ones," he snickered.

As early evening arrived, they found a dry spot where the bog's mist wasn't so thick. They needed to rest briefly, so they sat on the soft, dry patch. The bog humidity took its toll on them.

Each of them ate what they had in their packs. Lunar felt the most depleted.

"He should have drunk the milk," Sven told him.

But Ruddy handed him a mixture of berries. "These will help ya," he said happily.

Bluff attended to Epoch's wounds, which were healing nicely thanks to the balms given to them by Juxtus Lunder.

Akimu discovered an unusual ointment in a medicine bag. He handed it to Bluff, who opened the cap and smelled it. He jerked his head back instantly.

"Whew. Powerful stuff," he said. Akimu gestured to mix it with another ointment. Trusting the Flame Shadow's knowledge, Bluff did so, rubbing them onto Epoch's wounds. Epoch winced.

"Sorry, my friend. But this should help the healing process," he said, consoling the Giant. Epoch thanked him with a pat on the head.

Ahead of them, the marsh dipped into much more of a swamp. With a monocular, Haven looked far ahead through the murky surroundings. He saw a stretch of swamp riddled with tall grass, bushes, and trees. The water was green with duckweed. He assumed they would need to swim through it. He shook his head after inspecting it.

"There are deep waters ahead," He told the others. "We should reach higher grounds. There are cliffs ahead of us. We'll climb them to avoid swimming through the mire. Prepare yourselves for a climb."

As they entered a gorge, Lunar suggested they climb using a specific pulley system taught to him by his father. His people were excellent climbers, mainly living up in massive trees called White Colossus. The bark and leaves were white.

Using Lunar's pulley system, the ascent up the cliffs was manageable—even for Epoch, who was in terrible pain, still from the Xynd's arrows. Haven assisted each one to their feet as they reached the top. They found the ground flat, dry, and uninhabited, which brought relief, mainly since snakes inhabited the wet swamp below, as did leaches and snapping turtles—things they were happy to avoid.

They reached a thicket of Dark Plum Tree. Given their location, it was an unexpected find. The area felt cool, providing comfort. The dark trees bore fruit—delicious black plums, a favorite of Sven's. "We'll take some of these with us," Haven suggested to the Assemblage. "They'll provide extra nutrition. We should then find a place to rest. Do you have any thoughts?"

"I'd like to see what's beyond these trees," Bluff added. "The mountains are probably a day's journey ahead."

Haven agreed with a nod. Lunar, however, had already removed his things from his pack. He suggested that the location was ideal. Haven sighed as he saw the mountains in the distance but compromised when he saw Epoch wincing in pain. After all, his companions were exhausted, and the location was cool and dry.

As the group unpacked what they needed for the night, Haven walked further through the thicket of trees. They looked ancient, with dark branches and very few leaves. Some of them bore flowers, which he thought peculiar.

"Fruit and flowers?" He whispered. Ruddy followed him with a similar skepticism.

"Listen," Ruddy recommended, with his hand raised. A moment of silence passed by. "No sounds."

They exchanged looks of suspicion.

Haven pulled a plum off a branch. Plenty of them dangled within easy reach. "Bluff, come here," he called.

The insightful Drifter joined him. They each inspected the plum and then the trees. "The trees bear fruit, but the ones ahead of us still flower," Haven noted.

"It's as if they don't know the season," Bluff added.

Haven tossed the plum to Bluff. "It's fake."

"So are the ones over here," Ruddy added. They fell into an uncomfortable silence.

"I don't like it here," Haven quavered, his face creased with uncertainty.

Ruddy nodded and detected a disturbance. "The trees don't speak," he said.

"Trees speak?" Bluff asked, looking up through the branches.

"I've lived in trees my whole life," Ruddy said. "You and I use words and gestures to speak. Their language is chemical and scented." He sniffed the air. "These trees are not what they appear to be. This is a place of lies," he warned.

"We should get out of here," Haven said.

"Good idea," Bluff and Ruddy said in unison.

Haven walked ahead to see if there was a path out of the thicket. As he did, he walked into something unseen—a glass wall so clean and clear that none of them had noticed it. Hearing the thud, Bluff and Ruddy turned around. They squinted their eyes to see it. The others joined them there, fascinated by the unexpected oddness.

"A wall of glass?" Haven asked out loud.

Bluff shrugged his shoulders, short on insight. "I got nothing," he admitted.

Ruddy grazed his hand along it and walked a reasonable distance to his right but couldn't find where it ended. Lunar did the same on the other end. His glow reflected off it as he moved.

"Not sure how long it is," he shouted to the rest.

"We can always break our way through," Ruddy hinted.

"Now we're talking," Sven said. He lifted his axe. "I'm overdue for some breaking," he said, eager to do so. "Just one crash."

As he was about to swing, a feminine tune gave him pause. A woman of incredible beauty appeared on the other side. She swayed her hips with ease and intention. She whistled a soft tune they enjoyed.

The young men ogled at her attractiveness. She wore dark clothing that stressed her shape. Her long black hair added to her allure. She pressed her hand against the glass barrier.

Bluff placed his hand on top of hers, captivated by her beauty. He couldn't look away. Her eyes dazzled with colors of blue and gray. Her white skin appeared flawless, and her lips were red and lustrous. She stood confidently, her dark form-fitting clothes emphasizing her curves. The scent of her perfume filled the air, somehow wafting through the glass barrier.

They succumbed to her suggestive purpose. She knew it and smirked, looking at each one with a lustful glare. She had power over them and giggled with victory. Even Haven gave in to her enticement.

Akimu, however, suspected deceit, and it snapped him out of his lust. A woman of this beauty does not linger in such dark, strange places. He gained control of himself and inspected the height of the glass instead. He then looked down at the woman's feet. He noticed the ground at her feet appeared softer and fresher than the ground he stood on. His gut told him the glass provided some illusion.

She spoke to them mesmerizingly: "How pleasant it is to find strong, handsome men in such a lonely place. I'm a frightened girl. Help me." She then puckered her lips.

Akimu rolled his eyes and searched through the bag of tricks.

"I've come all this way, my lady, just to help you," Sven told her. She smiled at the short Viking. "How sweet. I am a queen without her king." She giggled. "Are you him?"

During this flirtation, Akimu grabbed a smoke grenade from the bag. He took it without Haven's notice, pulled the pin, and tossed it over the glass wall. It erupted into a cloud of smoke, and she screamed.

"What did you do?" Sven shouted angrily, ready to strike Akimu.

But to their shock, an ambush awaited them. The seven turned around to find several robbers raiding their packs and bags.

"They're taking our stuff!" Lunar shouted.

The robbers then darted off in opposite directions, holding on to what they could.

It was then that a group of filthy men with wooden weapons ambushed the seven. The Assemblage was quick to defend themselves, grabbing their weapons of choice. Haven used his crook, Ruddy his sling, Sven his ax, Epoch his fists, Bluff used his red staff, Lunar his sword, and Akimu his martial arts.

Recalling the fighting techniques Gamba had taught them just days earlier, the fight was theirs. They deflected every attack from the robbers, who were weak, clumsy, and slow. This gang of Kremin robbers lacked discipline and combat skills. They were men of treason and schemes, not of contest or battle.

Haven clashed with one of them, prevailing over him using his crook to bash the man's head. Another man advanced, swinging at him with a sword. So Haven grabbed his.

His sword clashed fiercely with the opponent's blade, each strike ringing with a metallic spark. The skilled swordsman moved with impressive grace and precision, forcing Haven to parry and dodge with all his might.

Sweat dripped from their brows as they circled each other, blades flashing under the evening light. Haven's heart pounded, his muscles straining with every swing and block. His opponent pressed hard, his attacks relentless, driving Haven back with each strike.

But Haven found his rhythm. He anticipated his adversary's moves, finding openings where none seemed possible. With a deft feint and quick sidestep, he broke through the swordsman's defenses, his blade slicing through the air with a decisive finality. The duel ended in a breathless moment, Haven standing victorious. His opponent's sword clattered to the ground.

The man found himself cut severely at the neck. He covered the wound with his hand and dashed into the woods beyond.

The skirmish was over, and the other filthy bog men cowered before retreating. Only one remained, who Haven had clocked over the head. The man lay on the ground, knocked out.

Behind the glass wall, the smoke cleared away. The woman's beauty and allure dripped down her face. A mask of makeup was her beauty. Haven curled his lip, disappointed that he fell for her treacherous trap. He hit the top of the glass filter with his crook.

"Stand back!" he cried out to the others.

After three hits, the wall shattered to the ground. Without its trick of softness, her actual age became clear. Her wrinkled skin and tiredness were clear without the glossy filter of the glass. Her fake beauty had become fully exposed.

The woman, whom the robbers called Queen Crave, sat on the ground sniveling. Her humiliation was apparent as the young men looked down at her. They realized that their brief tiff with her was based on deceit. She begged for their pity.

"Don't look at me! Don't look at me!" she cried, covering her face.

Sven looked over at their supplies. "They took our food and some of our packs. We should chase them down!"

Haven turned to the one robber, who was waking from his daze. Haven nudged him. "Wake up!"

The man awoke to see himself surrounded by the seven.

"An honor-less man taking what is not his. What say you?" Sven shouted.

"All I wanted was some food. Please don't hurt a harmless, infirm man," he cried.

"Harmless? I think not." Haven yelled with disdain. "Where have they taken our things?"

"How would I know? Those who stole from you live in the swamp with the snakes. Murkbreath, that's who they are," he explained, with his hands clenched together in a begging posture. "They are leeches. I was here to warn you."

"You're a serpent!" Sven shrieked, held back from striking him by Akimu.

"If you're not one of these Murkbreaths, who are you?" Bluff demanded, spitting at the old man.

"I'm a poor man in need. Please take care of me," he begged as he slowly reached for a knife from his boot. Bluff saw the old man's intent and kicked the man's boot. The knife fell to the ground. Ruddy responded with his slingshot. He shot a rock and hit the knife with a loud strike. It slid across the grass. One more shot sent it off the side of the cliff into the swamp below.

"No!" the old robber yelped. "Curse you!"

Bluff and Akimu tied the old man and woman up at the hands and then together at the wrists, making them sit down with their backs to each other. The seven grabbed what remained of their supplies, which wasn't much.

As they walked by the old woman, she kept calling out to them,

"Please! Tell me I'm beautiful! Want me! Want me!"

Each one ignored her as they walked by. They resented her, not for her old age, but for her deceit. Out of compassion, Bluff spoke to her kindly. "Leave this awful place. Find a land filled with sunlight and truth."

Her reaction revealed her true emptiness. She spit at him and kicked her feet. "Don't tell me what to do! No man controls me!" she yelled and spat at him again. Shallow-hearted pride was her will. She was a slave to her irrational spirit. So they left her behind with the robber.

"You don't control me!" she proclaimed to ears that no longer listened. "I don't need men! No one does!" They left her bitter rant behind them and proceeded forward.

Though exhausted from the day's travels, they walked far from the dark trees. They found a comfortable spot for shelter, and Epoch started a campfire. They divvied up the supplies they had left evenly among themselves. Ruddy said they had enough food to get them to the Blind Mountains if they rationed. "We'll have to catch an animal or two to cook. Perhaps find some berries, too," he recommended.

If they traveled efficiently, they would reach the mountains and begin their ascent tomorrow.

"Let's enjoy flat land while we have it," Haven grumbled, exhausted. "Tomorrow morning, we should prepare our feet. Make sure what you wear is fit for climbing."

Sven nodded and tapped Lunar's foot. "How are your ankles?" Sven asked sincerely.

Lunar shrugged. "Better, thanks."

Sven nudged him with a gentle smile. "Pain will not conquer you."

Haven saw Lunar's worry, and Sven did as well. Haven then looked around at the others. The group was tired and intimidated by the mountains in front of them.

"I've heard of the black rams that live up there," Lunar recalled. "They are predator-type animals that eat meat rather than vegetation."

"The hawks are worse," Epoch remarked. "Large enough to lift even me. Talons twice the size of my head."

"They hunt in pairs: male and female. We won't stand a chance if they attack us," Ruddy alleged.

They all peered through the darkness of night, scared of what tomorrow would bring. A jackal howled in the distance. Bluff peaked his head up from the fire.

"A mountain jackal—" he started.

"That's enough!" Haven interrupted. "No more talk of danger. We are not boys who tell ghost stories. We are men prepared for what lies ahead. We have armor, weapons, medicines, and the knowledge of what it takes to reach the summit."

The Assemblage lifted their heads, turning to their leader. "You believe we can make it?" Ruddy asked, his face worn with fatigue.

"I know for certain we will make it," Haven declared angrily. "Two kings and a Geezer chose us. If they believe in us, so will I. Now, get sleep. Tomorrow, we have a stretch of wilderness to pass and climb mountains."

They acknowledged his plea for perseverance. His anger resonated, creating a noticeable tension in the air. The fire's light cast a spark into their eyes, kindling a decision to press on.

Haven stared into the flickering flames as his comrades fell asleep. He had demanded endurance from them, but doubt gnawed at his mind. Who was he to lead these brave souls into the jaws of danger? The mantle of leadership felt like a burden too significant to bear, each decision a precipice over an abyss.

The night grew cold; his mind refused to quiet. His thoughts drifted back to his father, whose memory was both a comfort and a torment. Haven's heart ached with a deep longing, a yearning for fatherly guidance. Sleep came fitfully, his dreams haunted by the memory of his father, Daniel, the man whose face he struggled to see.

15

ROCKWORM'S REACH

The seven approached the barren wilderness that separated them from the mountains, but first, they passed through dense, complicated woods with a mess of intertwining trees across the wood floor. Navigating the intricate web of gnarled roots proved challenging. Each step presented obstacles and twists that slowed their journey. Like resilient hands, the tree's roots guarded the territory, testing the patience of anyone who sought passage.

"We should have gone another way," Lunar complained.

"No way!" Ruddy exclaimed. "This is incredible." The others quickly noticed his fascination with the forest floor. "I know the floor is tricky to walk, but these are the trees of music," he added. "I have never heard their song before. Stand still and remain quiet. Let us listen."

The others were not interested in staying since many trees had branches reaching for them. But for Haven, he couldn't help but appreciate Ruddy's love of tree life.

"Okay, everyone. Stand still and hush," he ordered, happy to appease his feral friend.

"Oh, come on!" Sven protested. "The boy loves trees; we get it."

Haven gave him an angry stare. Sven sighed in response. The entire group paused silently, but they heard nothing. Ruddy raised his hand, signaling for patience. The others rolled their eyes. But sure enough, the trees rewarded Ruddy's curiosity. Within seconds, a peaceful note rang in the distance. And then another higher harmonizing note whistled past them. They all looked above, baffled by the sound.

Reverie fell over the seven as an orchestra of whistles, tings, and airy melodies floated through the leaves. Soft winds grazed the tiny instruments hanging from branches. The curvature of the oddly shaped and sturdy leaves created elegant sounds. Ruddy looked around at the others and smiled.

"That should be enough for memory to hold," Haven said. "Let's move forward, everyone."

Ruddy nodded excitedly. "Yes. I will not forget that."

But the serenity they enjoyed fell short. To everyone's surprise and amusement, a Blue Squirrel landed on Lunar's head. He found it horrifying, however.

"Help!" he cried. "Get it off me!"

Annoyed with the Pulveran's childlike behaviors, Sven yelled at him. "Oh, quiet, you wimp! It's just a squirrel."

"Get it off me, get it off me!" Lunar shrieked, swatting at the critter. He turned to the nearest person for help, which was Sven. Lunar lowered his head into a comedic panic, pleading for a helping hand. But in doing so, he tripped over a gnarl and fell straight into Sven. Both crashed into the gnarled wood floor.

The small Norseman grew hot with anger. He stood up with a hostile huff. "You fool!" he shouted, pushing glimmering Lunar off of him. He then grabbed the squirrel off Lunar and flung it into the woods.

"Get it off me!" Lunar still cried out.

"It's not on you anymore!" some others shouted. Lunar settled down, looking around for the squirrel, not realizing he had collided with Sven.

"You cry over a squirrel?" Sven shouted. "You, wuss!"

Lunar turned to the Norseman, still with a frightened expression.

"Sven," Haven said. "Calm down." But the Norseman would not.

"No, I've had it! Why are you even with us?" He huffed, meeting Lunar's eyes. "How will you fight the enemy when a small rodent frightens you?"

Lunar took offense and responded with a weak insult: "You're a rodent, you small want-to-be Viking!"

"What do you know?" Sven retaliated angrily. "You're afraid of a squirrel, you coward! That's all you are, a coward!"

A silence fell over the group. Lunar's expression was clear. He stepped back with his head down.

"Sven!" Haven yelled, his face flushed. "Both of you keep quiet and separate!"

Sven turned to Haven and agreed. "Yes. Good idea!" The others looked on, disappointed by the scuffle. The last thing they needed was a division among themselves, and Haven clarified it, pointing his finger at Sven and then at Lunar.

"Keep focused!" He yelled in a gravelly voice. "Lunar, you're with me at the front."

The others understood it clearly, but Sven would need time. He kept quiet and to himself in the back by Epoch.

Lunar kept his head down, joining Haven at the front. He knew his cowardly action brought shame to himself. But hearing it from his brave friend was difficult to accept. Despite the feud, Haven led them onward.

~ ~ ~

After leaving the gnarled woods behind them, beauty presented itself. The seven emerged, finding a river. They were desperate for cooling waters.

"Beautiful," Bluff said with gleaming eyes.

Green, vibrant trees accompanied the river's edge. The babbling sounds of running water pleased their hearts as they entered it. They considered it a gift of creation. Each took turns dipping their heads. Epoch gave in to his excitement and cannonballed.

Their laughter and shouts of joy rang along the banks as they splashed and frolicked. The sensation of the crisp water against their skin brought a renewed sense of vitality and camaraderie among them, washing away the fatigue of their travels and the hardened mud that covered their uniforms.

But something unexpected roamed the refreshing waters. As they stepped out of the river onto the other side, their presumption of peace exposed them to a terrible danger. Rope-like objects emerged from the river's floor. With eyes darting, Bluff was the first to realize what they were.

"The roots of Snarlag!" He cried out, quick to discern the tentacles' origin.

"Watch out!" Haven cried. "She's found us!"

They recalled what Gamba and Jehu told them on the plains of San Hadza. The rockworms' appendages grew in many places throughout the island. It turned out that they, too, had supplanted themselves firmly into the bedrock of this river. Several serpentine appendages erupted from the depths, whipping through the air.

Each one, thick and muscular, thrashed with a mind of its own, attempting to trap them with their deadly grasp. Stunned by their speed, the seven sought to defend themselves, their training coming to the forefront as they dodged and struck the flailing roots.

Moving like snakes, the roots shot rapidly across the water, pulling the seven deep into the river. Their undulated movements were difficult to predict. Sven drew his axe and swung with fierce precision but could not keep up with the sinuous motions. A root slithered across the water and knocked him onto the shore. His horned helmet stuck on the rocky shore.

While Sven struggled to rise, Lunar acted vigilantly, stabbing his small, sharp sword into the root that struck Sven. He called out proudly, "I got it! I got it, Sven!" But a twisting root wrapped around his legs and pulled him beneath the churning water. Sven stood but was too late to help him.

The others combated with other appendages. Each was engaged by separate roots, which moved relentlessly, maneuvering wildly, and proved challenging to predict.

Haven and Bluff stood back to back, waist-high in the water. Their movements synchronized as they sliced through the air, cutting down the snaking roots that lashed out at them. Despite their resilient efforts, more roots emerged, making it laborious to keep up.

Epoch and Akimu fought beside each other. Epoch hoisted Akimu into the air with a mighty heave, allowing him to slice an incoming root cleanly in half as he soared upward.

Another erupted from the water. Epoch grabbed hold of it, squeezing it tightly. But the root wrapped around his waist, lifting him from the water. Bluff swung his red staff and pierced it, causing it to split into two halves. This freed Epoch, who fell back into the water to deal with the next one he could find.

Still, on shore, Sven fought thinner roots tangled around him like vines. He shouted for help, but as they tightened their grip, he lost breath. Ruddy shot out from the river, trying to reach him, but a root held him at the foot, tugging him backward. He fired his slingshot and broke a vine that wrapped around Sven's neck. Once again able to breathe, Sven wiggled his arm free and wielded his axe, slicing at the remaining roots.

After piercing many roots, the remaining ones returned to the water and rocks they came from. Panic surged through Bluff as one last root burst from the waters, coiling around his ankle with relentless force. His fingers clawed at the riverbank in a desperate effort to escape. He pled for help, reaching out to Haven, but it was too late. Bluff took a final breath before he descended into the river.

Haven, Epoch, and Akimu searched the waters to rescue him. Ruddy readied his slingshot, trying to find where he could fire.

Sven paced up and down the riverside. He rushed to the water's edge. "Lunar!" He shouted, dropping his shield and axe.

As Haven, Epoch, and Akimu emerged from the water onto the shore, each desperate for air, the frantic shouts and splashes ceased. They stood there, speechless. The air hung heavy with disbelief, each grappling with what unfolded. They searched the water's surface but saw nothing.

"Lunar! Bluff!" Ruddy called out.

"Lunar's gone too?" Haven asked, eyebrows raised and pulled together.

Epoch shook his head, uncertain. With no sign of their friends, they met up at a spot on shore close to where it had all happened.

Akimu returned to the group holding Bluff's erokan—a valuable article Bluff would not choose to travel without. He handed it to Haven. Words failed them as they stood there staring at it. Once Epoch saw it, he cried out angrily.

"Any sign of Lunar?" Sven asked, but no one responded. "Lunar!" He shouted again at the water.

The others lowered their heads in defeat. Sven screamed and pulled off his vest to tear his outer garment. He fell to his knees, seething. "What sort of evil does this?"

He looked out across the river. "I will kill it this day. Fight me, fight me, you beast! Fight me!" Sven ran back into the river, daring Snarlag to raise her appendages again.

Ruddy called out to him, but Haven silenced him. "Give him his rage."

Returning to shore, Sven wept for his lost brothers. There, they learned quickly that grief is an enemy's weapon.

The five walked both sides of the waters once more. Time passed quickly, however, and Haven knew they had to continue their journey. Especially since the ground rumbled, reminding them of their enemy in the mountains.

Epoch wore Bluff's erokan around his neck. Sven, who found Lunar's shield a ways down the river, brought it to a rocky bank at a curve. He took the shield and stuck it in the ground as a monument.

Haven shed a tear seeing Bluff's erokan hang from Epoch's neck. He then felt his own necklace—the green pendant his father had given him many years ago. And he recalled the words Gamba told him, "Your father offered you a choice. A path to choose for yourself—one of pain or one of healing."

In that lonely silence, they knew not what to say, their hearts heavy with the absence of their friends. With his axe and shield behind him, Sven lowered his head and closed his eyes. Collecting his thoughts, he recited a Norseman dirge:

"Death is an enemy taking those we hold dear.
We toss and turn; we grieve, awake and restless.
Only the dead know true sleep."

"A PATH TO CHOOSE FOR YOURSELF—
ONE OF PAIN OR ONE OF HEALING."

16

CLIMB

The five marched toward the mountains with heavy hearts and silent mouths. Each face bore the indelible marks of sorrow, silently expressing shared grief as they marched onward.

A vast, desolate, fog-shrouded terrain lay between them and the imposing mountains. The dense, swirling mountain mist enveloped the surroundings like a canopy. They understood this stretch of land to be called the Misty Badlands.

Unphased by the distant cries of soaring hawks—their thoughts remained on Bluff and Lunar. During their darkest moments, they leaned on each other for support. With the future path ahead like a shroud of secrecy, Haven led them, intent on reaching their destination. Below the haze, they navigated, remaining steadfast.

During their approach, they found a wooden sign spiked into the ground that read, 'Death is ahead of you.' Ruddy gulped before looking to Haven, whose neck and jaw tightened.

"This is no option," he said coldly. "We keep going. We're men."

Sven looked up and pounded his chest. "Time to conquer what others cannot."

They pressed on, undeterred by the poisonous things that crawled on the ground beneath them. The thought of turning back never once crossed their minds.

Haven narrowed his eyes, peering up at the mountains before entering them. The sharp peaks disappeared into swirling clouds. "Blind cliffs do not scare me," he hissed.

The mountains loomed large. They stepped cautiously, with the crunch of brittle rock beneath their boots. The foothills were foreboding, with dead skeletal trees clinging precariously to stones. The path ahead was winding, littered with sharp outcrops and hidden crevices threatening to trip the unwary.

As they ascended further into the mist, the world around them shifted and warped, and each one's boundaries of reality blurred. The fog played tricks on their senses, as did breathing in the high altitudes. Distorting shapes and sounds kept them on edge as they scanned the area for dangers. Amidst this uncertainty, they kept checking their weapons, strapped securely to their sides.

Epoch called out, pointing ahead. Scattered across the rocky ground were the remains of other travelers. Tattered clothing and broken weapons lay among bones, the remnants of those who had attempted the perilous journey before them.

Haven's stomach sank as he kneeled beside a rusted helmet, its surface marred by deep scratches, which only a large animal could inflict. Akimu moved closer, his face grim. He picked up a fractured shield, its insignia barely recognizable under layers of grime and decay. Sven stood silently, his pale face reflecting the somber mood. He bowed his head to pay respects.

"These poor souls," Ruddy muttered, kicking aside a crumbling breastplate. "They were attacked. But by what?"

Haven straightened, his jaw set. He would not allow his comrades to share the same fate. "We must move on," he said, his voice firm. "We will not speculate. Instead, we'll honor their memory by succeeding where they fell." They stepped over the remnants of the past, marching forward to conquer the blind peaks ahead.

Again, Haven's thoughts wandered to his father, a man, like the mountains, shrouded in mystery. Looking around, he remembered all his mother had told him. In these moments of quiet reflection, he delved deep into his memories, searching for clues, drawing strength from the untold stories he wanted to know. He journeyed to save Wunduria and to connect with his heroic purpose, seeking his father's legacy. *He wanted me to be a refuge for the innocent. I will be that hero.*

They climbed, assisting one another through many obstacles, navigating steep inclines, and avoiding unsteady rock ledges. They were not just survivors of a dangerous quest but warriors ready to face whatever challenges lay ahead.

The air grew colder with every step. They stopped to fill their canteens at a fresh spring. Epoch drank and drank. The rest chewed on venison jerky and continually looked ahead.

The five climbed up and up, higher and higher. They had a testy way about them. An uncontrollable fury that propelled them onward. Epoch and Sven traveled violently, kicking aside and knocking over anything in their paths. Sven announced his resolve to kill the great worm and avenge his friends' death.

Once or twice, he would overtake Haven's lead. The Norseman stomped every way he went. Haven decided not to challenge him, knowing all men grieved differently. The others took notice and honored Sven's gloom.

They saw wreckage and debris from old skyships, reminders that these mountains were too dangerous to travel by air. This became increasingly obvious the higher they went. The winds became a terrible obstacle, compromising their footing. Each feared tumbling down the mountainside into the unknown. The constant rumbling of the ground below their feet gave new meaning to "the Moving Mountains." It also reminded them they were closer than ever to Snarlag, the great rockworm.

They kept their shields on their backs and helmets on their heads to protect themselves from falling rocks. The long coats Emmy had given them proved helpful, each keeping them warm.

They settled for a moment in a dark and lonely place. They set their supplies down to rest on a precipice one thousand feet high. All five gazed at what lay ahead of them—a lonely haze. The brooding view increased the uncertainty of their quest. Their five forlorn figures stared into the emptiness. Each questioned their value in silence. *Can I be what I need to be?*

Haven accepted a sad possibility in his heart: all they had accomplished and suffered would most likely go untold. Their quest was desperate—far more so with their friends gone. He looked out into the blur, recalling all those who had mocked them along their travels. They were the very ones he was trying to save.

He wondered if this was just part of manhood: to be hated by those you help and ignored by the ones you save. The obscurity of the Blind Mountains hardened his heart. He recalled the words of Gamba Tru, "It is not the mountain you must conquer, but it is yourself." He closed his eyes and allowed an irritable temper to rise within him. His coat swayed in the wind as he stared into the miles of unknown in front of him.

"Let's leave this place behind," He lamented.

~ ~ ~

The second day of climbing was harsher. They traversed mountain passes despite the worsening winds and visibility. Seeing each other proved difficult, even though they were only feet apart. They whistled in succession to keep sense of one another's whereabouts. Two earthquakes occurred, and constant soft rumbles in between. Their enemy was indeed awakening.

An unknown, fierce mountain beast fell upon them. It stood tall on all fours, taller than most of them. They drew their weapons, ready to battle it, but how could they fight what they could barely see? The animal's grunting and clamoring hooves gave away its location a bit. They turned their heads this way and that way, trying to find it.

Ruddy readied his slingshot, but before he shot a pellet, the animal charged him, pitting him against a rock wall. Sven was the first to attack it, pulling out a hatchet from his side. But the creature was quicker. It knocked him to the ground, sending him off the cliff. Many of his things fell into the misty abyss below. Epoch grabbed hold of him before he, too, fell into it.

Akimu activated his cloak and disappeared. As the beast lunged forward, Haven pierced it with the point of his crook, parrying its powerful horn strikes with quick swings. Epoch aimed for its vulnerable flanks, striking its side with his fists.

The beast roared, and its heavy hooves thundered against the rocky floor.

"Akimu! Now!" Haven commanded, hoping the Flame Shadow was ready to attack. Indeed, he was. Akimu swung his fire daggers at the beast. Once inside its flesh, he ignited them. The beast made a sound of anguish that distressed them all. Ultimately, Akimu's attack killed the beast. He, Epoch, and Haven rolled it off the cliff's edge to ensure its death.

"What was that thing?" Sven grumbled, rubbing his chest, which had taken the brunt of the beast's force.

Ruddy stood, straightening his helmet. "I don't know, but it hit me hard. My head hurts."

"Perhaps we shouldn't whistle," Haven suggested. "Let's tie ourselves together with a rope."

Ruddy nodded. "Good idea. Like the mountaineers do."

From then on, they traveled roped together. They continued up and over mountain passes. Shrill winds came down quickly from the gray blur above them. In every direction they looked, all they saw was the thick haze. The blur was so encompassing that they wondered if they were traveling in the right direction. Haven trusted Ruddy's internal compass, but even he felt unsure on multiple occasions.

The mountains proved perilous. They climbed dangerous paths, some of which led to awful places. Haven wondered if it was possible to reach the summit in such conditions.

He eventually thought of his treehome back in San Hadza. For a brief moment, he smiled, thinking of the woods, small rivers, and fields. He also thought of his mother and Thunder, his graceful horse. He hoped dearly to see them again.

Again, night fell upon the five. The wind was fiercer and colder than the night before. Thankfully, Epoch noticed a cave, so they went inside it. To their surprise, several small goats rested there. Sven suggested killing and eating one, but the rest thought it was a waste of energy, seeing that there wasn't enough wood to make a sufficient fire for cooking.

"Chew your dry venison," Ruddy suggested.

It started raining, a nasty cold wetness. The cave protected them from the elements. Even the air cleared up a bit within it. They saw each other's faces clearly for the first time all day. Haven built a small fire with what useful things he could find to burn. They warmed the last of the beans they had.

Despite the improved visibility and a meal in their stomachs, the night felt glum. This bleakness prompted an intense sadness that filled their hearts. Each of them recalled a memory of their fallen brothers. After Sven shared his memory, he stood overcome by anguish and walked to the cave's entrance. He looked out into the dark mist.

"These cursed mountains. Is it not enough for them to be cold? They must blind us too?" He turned to the others and admitted his regret concerning Lunar. "Brothers, I am lost in my guilt. I called him a coward. But he fought for me when I fell. He showed courage."

The wind entered the cave and blew their small fire out. The darkness mocked them. Akimu soon brought the fire back, but the flame was unwilling to give much light. Sven sat down next to him.

"In this cave, light is precious," said Sven. "Lunar was a light in dark places, a friend in dreary times."

~ ~ ~

A long night of rain made the ground slippery. The five climbed another mountain range, slipping many times. Fueled by revenge, they repeatedly blamed Snarlag for all their troubles, voicing their anger as motivation. The thing was, though, they didn't know how to kill her. Snarlag's skin was as tough as the rock on the mountainside.

"How do we penetrate such an outer shell?" Sven asked, but no one answered the question.

Ruddy asked Haven how he planned to kill her, but he didn't have an answer to give. His response was more of a demand. "We must get there first if we are to kill her."

"Maybe one of those grenades will penetrate its skin?" Ruddy suggested. "We saw what they did to the Xynd."

Sven shrunk back and reluctantly confessed. "They fell off the cliff yesterday."

"What?" Ruddy yelped.

"I almost fell off the cliff, too, ya know," he replied defensively. "That beast nearly killed me!"

"I'm sure they have explosives at the summit," Haven said, short on patience.

"That's if the armies get there," Epoch said disparagingly.

But instead of reasoning, their frustration mounted. They cast anxious glances toward the mountain peak as the winds worsened. Knowing not how to express his frustration, Epoch lifted a rock twice the size of Sven and threw it over the cliff's edge. He about had it with obstacles.

"I hate this place!" he boomed.

Sven took sips from his flask, sending his anger into a belligerent speech. Ruddy retaliated by calling the Norseman many bad things. They almost came to blows.

But a thunderstorm rolled in above them with heavy rains that hit them sideways. Even some hail fell upon them. They fastened their helmets tighter, keeping their heads low. Even with their gear and heavy clothing, they shivered from the cold. It drenched them from head to toe. Their thick, long coats flapped wildly in the wind. The storm's harshness broke down their spirits. Then came the lightning, which struck violently again and again.

"We need to find cover!" Haven shouted, looking over his shoulder into the mist, hoping his comrades were still behind him.

"Any inns and pubs nearby?" Ruddy remarked. "A pint of beer would be nice right now."

CLIMB

They huddled under a rocky overhang, exhausted, heaving breaths in the high altitude. With few options, Haven advised what seemed most logical: "We'll stay here until the storm calms." But their cover was short-lived. Lightning struck the rocky overhang, and it crumbled on top of them. They fell under the weight of the rocks—a punishing hit to the ground.

Under the rubble, they lay cold, wet, and further injured. Each called out, hoping all to be alive. Epoch soon freed himself of the rubble's weight. He lifted whatever he could off the others. Coupled with their strength, they freed themselves. Each bleeding and bruised, they again retreated to a spot clear of ruin.

"I'm open to ideas!" Haven yelled. The wind continued to press against the mountainside, chilling them to their bones. They shook and held on to one another.

Finally, frustrated beyond control, Epoch punched the rock wall they stood against. But the impact of his first hit made an unexpected sound—a hollow thud. The other four turned around the moment they heard it. Epoch glanced at Haven with narrowed eyes. This time, Akimu pounded his fist against it. Again, a hollow thud.

"It's hollow?" Haven asked, pushing his hand against it.

Epoch raised his fists and punched the wall again with more force. They were stunned to discover that the wall gave way. Startled by a fierce strike of lightning, they all started hitting it, perplexed that this portion of the mountainside was artificial.

After forcing it open, they entered an empty passageway and discovered a tunnel. Akimu ignited one of his fire daggers, lighting up the emptiness before them. They proceeded silently, stepping slowly across the wet and slippery rock floor. Sven slipped to the ground clumsily, but none could blame him.

"Thanks for punching the mountain," Ruddy said to Epoch.

He looked down at his little friend and smiled. "Sometimes you just gotta punch something."

"I agree," Sven said, climbing to his feet.

Intrigued by the unknown, they treaded the tunnel cautiously. Akimu held his fire dagger out in front of them, casting light down the passageway, which, with walls lined with smooth ancient stone, seemed to whisper tales of forgotten history.

"Where are we?" Sven wondered, squinting into the darkness.

Ruddy, who pulled a strawberry from one of his pouches, replied matter-of-factly. "Inside a mountain."

"Give me one of your strawberries," Sven replied.

Haven shushed them, concerned about what lay ahead.

They ventured deeper into the tunnel, their senses heightened. The enclosed space seemed to magnify every little sound. Drips echoed, and the howling winds behind them hissed.

As they approached the end of the tunnel, they saw a door adorned with unknown symbols and ancient runes. The door's surface shimmered with unexplainable energy, and the anticipation of what lay beyond it was almost unbearable.

"A door inside a mountain," Haven said softly.

"I wonder what's on the other side," Sven added, biting his nails.

They all exchanged cautious glances, wondering if they should unravel the secrets hidden on the other side. With a collective breath, they reached out to touch the door, their fingers brushing against the cold surface as they wanted to enter the unknown.

"How does a door get inside a mountain?" Epoch asked.

Sven gave it a closer look. "It's well constructed. Someone built this."

Ruddy placed his hand over his face, shaking his head. "Of course, someone built it, you idiot," he replied. "A door just doesn't grow inside a mountain."

Before Sven could snap back with an angered response, Akimu knocked on the door loudly. After a little while, he knocked once more. They heard a metallic scraping noise, like a drawbar lifting from its slot. Sven put his hand on the handle of his axe in case danger lurked on the other side. The others prepared their weapons, too.

"Let's hope they want company," Ruddy remarked.

The door opened slightly, and someone peeked outside at them. Haven tried to look through the crack but could not distinguish the face. "Hello, we need shelter," he pleaded, holding his crook close before himself.

A Mountain Dweller inspected them from the other side. She assessed them silently before speaking. "Who you?" she asked, her voice carrying a hint of wariness but with a willingness to listen.

"Who you?" Sven repeated with a crinkled face.

Haven spoke with slight nervousness. "We are travelers on a quest to reach the Breathing Summit. We are lost," he trembled, shaking, still wet and cold.

After listening intently, the Mountain Dweller's expression hardened, and without a word, she shut the door, leaving the five uncertain of what was to come.

"Was it something I said?" Haven asked. A baffled Akimu shrugged.

When murmuring emanated from behind the closed door, their curiosity piqued. The five waited, all shivering in anticipation.

The door opened again, revealing the Mountain Dweller's eyes. She fixed her gaze on them and inquired, "What names?"

The five tried to understand what the girl was asking. Haven answered quickly.

"I am Haven," he replied slowly. "The others are—"

The door swung open, revealing a small girl beckoning them to follow. "Chase me!" she exclaimed in a squeaky voice. She hurriedly fled a tunnel with a second Mountain Dweller running ahead. Ignited with urgency, Haven and the others all shuffled in one after the other without a clue of what to conclude.

She led them through many tunnels that twisted and turned endlessly. Even if they tried, none of them could find their way back.

Her tiny stature and dust-covered appearance exuded a durable aura, speaking of a life spent navigating the subterranean channels she raced through. Her explanations poured forth like a rushing river. Each word suggested a grand and noble purpose awaiting their arrival.

The one in front of her kept scurrying faster. "Hurry!" she'd urge. "Faster!"

The five found it challenging to keep up. Their armor and gear clinked as they followed the two tiny girls. Haven kept his eyes forward and wide, his excitement building with each hurried step. *What awaits us? Where are we running to?*

His comrades huffed, nearly out of breath.

"Where are we going?" Sven asked.

"How would I know?" Ruddy replied.

"I wasn't asking you!"

They passed through a channel with water flowing down both sides. Plant life dangled above them. The beauty dazzled each one, except for Epoch, who lowered his head, dodging the vines and flowers. He sneezed mightily, passing through them.

They then emerged into a vast cavern illuminated by softly glowing crystals, revealing a bustling community of small Mountain Dwellers. Curious glances greeted the five there, as did hopeful faces illuminated with awe. The two tiny girls gestured for them to walk to the heart of the cavern, where a gathering of elders and warriors awaited their arrival.

The atmosphere crackled with energy and expectation, leaving Haven cautiously optimistic. He was eager to discover the secrets that awaited him in this unfamiliar underground world. He looked up at those who awaited them.

On a platform only a few steps high, nine elders stood in a straight horizontal row, their figures draped in flowing capes that billowed slightly in the underground breeze. Clad in attire that spoke of ancient traditions and authority, Haven took them for those akin to clergy or revered leaders. Their eyes fixed on him with what he discerned as scrutiny.

Dim orange light emanated from the floor, casting a warm glow to rise like hazy flames, while beams of light filtered down from the rocky crystal cavern ceiling. It was no longer cold, but a warmth rose from the floor. A welcoming change for the five.

In front of these elders, six Mountain Dweller Guards sat in respectful silence, their faces steady and focused. Epoch, Akimu, Sven, and Ruddy looked above at the heights of their surroundings. The ambiance of the cavern added to the sense of solemnity within this hidden world inside the mountain.

Amidst this captivating scene, a tenth elder stepped forward from the center of the row, his movements deliberate and commanding. His attention focused on the five. Nothing about his clothing separated him from the other nine elders. Haven speculated about whether he had a higher rank than the others. *Is he their king?*

"Which you, Haven?" this tenth elder asked, his high voice echoing through the cavern. Their dialect was rudimentary, but Haven understood the question.

Among gasps and whispers from the hundreds of surrounding mountain-dwelling spectators, he stepped forward, his eyes darting from side to side. He lifted his head, keeping his crook in front of him. "I-I am. I, Haven." He muttered, pointing to himself.

The commotion of gasps and whispers increased in multitude and volume. Even certain elders whispered to each other, but the lead elder lifted his hand. "Quiet, quiet!" He commanded.

Immediately, silence returned. "Bring others!" He ordered a burly servant, who sprinted off through the crowd.

Looking past the warriors and at the lead elder, Haven implored him. "Where are we?"

The man raised an eyebrow and looked out at the crowds. "Dritt kingdom. Unknown, hidden, we live." He replied assuredly. "We Dritt. Home Undar."

The burly servant returned, navigating through the multitude of people. His movements were quick and purposeful. He guided others toward the five. The crowd of spectators parted, turning to follow their progress. He exited the crowd and brought two others to Haven.

"Your friends." The tenth elder said, aglow with pleasantness.

Haven turned around to find what he thought was impossible. Speedily approaching him, Bluff and Lunar ran out from the crowd, calling out to their comrades.

"Bluff?" Haven uttered, choking up with tears. Their faces instantly transformed into expressions of unguarded relief.

Sven's face lit up as he found his albino friend alive. "Lunar!" He cried, surging forward. He enveloped Lunar in a robust embrace.

The crowd of mountain dwellers erupted into applause. The seven rejoiced, showing everyone who watched that their reunion was special. The Assemblage hugged one another repeatedly, and the Dritt elders watched joyfully.

Standing on his tiptoes, Sven grabbed Lunar's face and kissed his cheeks. "In the light of day, you were lost! But within a mountain, I found you!" It was a stark contrast to their usual bickering from days prior. Lunar welcomed the brotherly affection. He even enjoyed the back-thumping embrace of his Norseman friend.

The air filled with laughter and jubilation. The bond of brotherhood was palpable. Emotion blinded them to their surroundings as they forgot for a moment where they were.

"Bluff!" Epoch boomed, lifting the Drifter from the ground for an emotional hug. They both held excited smiles. Epoch lifted Bluff far above himself. "My friend, my brother!"

Epoch placed the erokan he had saved back onto Bluff's head. His excitement increased. "You found it! Thank you!" he cried, putting it back around his forehead.

The crowd of mountain-dwelling Dritts' applause drifted into silence. The ground rumbled, and dust fell from the cavern's rocky ceiling.

The seven turned their attention to the reverent Dritt elders. "We thank you," Haven began, standing beside Bluff again. "You have united us!"

The onlooking lead elder raised his hand, pointing above. "Dangerous worm awakes." He declared. "You save Undar. You save Dritts. We bring you Summit."

Haven turned to Bluff with a smirking stare. "Looks like we're back at it."

Bluff smiled. "To the summit, we go."

17

THE SUMMIT

Reunited, the Assemblage ascended a spiral tunnel from the subterranean depths of Undar. Two Dritt Liaisons led the way, scurrying in front of them. The surge of adrenaline in each young man was not just their own, but a combined pulse as the noises from above reached their ears. The clashing of metals, the shouts of rallying troops, and the rhythmic drumming of war drums grew louder and louder.

Their faces revealed nervousness as they emerged from the twisting and turning tunnel. They left apprehension behind them, stepping into the exhilarating honor of duty. Their eyes met the manliest of scenes.

Amidst the clang of hammers and the crackling of fires, Viking blacksmiths towered over all the other kingdom's men, working alongside the Hadzians.

The Vikings were tall and broad, renowned for their muscular bodies and meat-rich diets. Their hair and beards were equally impressive, often flowing, braided, or styled into intricate patterns, further adding to their imposing appearance. Even their allies feared them.

These tall and mighty Vikings toiled tirelessly in the harsh elements of the cold mountaintop. With muscles honed by a life of physical labor, these Norsemen hewed massive blocks of Blyer Stone and other materials, smelting them into formidable weapons of war, such as swords, axes, spears, and shields.

The seven young men looked with awe, intimidated by their new surroundings.

"They're gigantic," Ruddy gulped.

Lunar stood frozen by intimidation. "Which one?" he asked, with an increasing frown.

"All of them."

As they stepped further onto the mountaintop, an unusual motion greeted them—the ground seemed to breathe beneath their feet; its slow and steady rise and fall was proof of the ancient power that lay dormant within.

Each noticed the many cracks that spread across the summit floor. Snarlag's breath rose through them in various hues—like a rainbow evaporating into the mist. The ground lifted with each exhale, like the belly of a purring cat. The cracks expanded in size and then tightened with each breath.

Haven stood beside his team with brave energy. They beheld the sprawling encampment spread out before them. Many battalions of soldiers moved with ambition, their armor gleaming in the soft light as they readied themselves for the impending battle.

Sven stepped up and pushed his way between Ruddy and Lunar. "Oh, come on. These Vikings aren't that big." He stepped out ahead of his comrades, returning to face them. He opened his arms wide, thrilled to be among his native people. "We can run with these guys!" He boasted. "Nothing can stop us!"

As the words left his mouth, a squad of Viking Berserkers marched through him, knocking him to the ground.

Bluff cringed. "Oh."

Haven closed his eyes and shook his head. Come on, Sven. "You're in their way!" He shouted at him.

The Berserkers ran by, and the trampled Sven lay on his back. He looked up into the cloudy skies above him and wearily managed a slight sound of hurt. As his comrades stood there wondering if he was okay, he coughed up dirt. Lunar and Ruddy ran over to him, staring down into his face.

"Good thing you had your helmet on," Lunar chimed, watching Sven blink several times. Ruddy helped him stand, and they walked him back to the others.

A Hadzian soldier rushed up toward them, calling for their identity. "Are you that band of young warriors the King sent us?"

Haven stepped forward. "Yes. We are the Assemblage who vowed—."

"Which one of you is the shepherd?" the soldier interrupted.

"That is me," Haven stuttered.

"Alright," the Hadzian soldier replied with a condescending look. He inspected them up and down with scrutiny until his eyes fell upon Epoch. "I'm surprised you all made it up here alive. Or did that Giant carry you?" he sneered. "Follow me."

The seven turned to follow him, but the soldier halted them immediately. "Just the shepherd," he informed them.

Haven looked at his comrades, tilting his head. "If I go, we all go," he demanded.

To his right, Akimu crossed his shoulders and lifted his chin, staring back at the Hadzian soldier with a solid stature.

The soldier huffed. "Very well. Just keep up."

They followed him through the busy camp, weaving through the organized chaos of Viking Miners and Hadzian Archers. The seven young men thrummed with excitement as they ran along.

"It's awkward to run on moving ground," Lunar told Ruddy. "It moves like the sea with a rainbow of colors."

The Hadzian soldier yelled back at them. "Do not be misled. Snarlag's breath is beautiful, but she is not. She's taken hundreds of us already with her roots. Keep your eye out for them. They attack randomly."

Haven kept his attention only on the soldier who led the way. He found relief in the guide's steely resolve, which inspired him and reminded him there was truth and purpose to their quest. Rushing beyond the encampments, they approached a meeting of generals, a gathering of formidable leaders from the kingdoms of Wunduria.

Jagged rocks and sparse clumps of grass surrounded these generals. A gust of howling wind parted the mist, revealing breathtaking views of the mountains beyond them. It was then that Haven saw a more significant extent of his surroundings. To his right, the summit itself provided a natural amphitheater of stone. In its walls were ancient carvings and a doorway.

The Hadzian soldier addressed his commanding officer: "Sir, here are the young men sent to us by the King."

Grouped behind the soldier, the Assemblage took their stance. Ahead of them, gathered in a spectral haze, they watched the five generals standing resolute in their command. One of them looked over his shoulder with interest. He stepped out of the ethereal vapor and into a clearer view. This general was Hadzian, dressed in copper armor and green gambeson cloth.

"Is the shepherd with them?" he asked.

"Yes, sir," the soldier replied. "He preferred the others join him."

"Very well."

Taking a step forward, Haven lifted his crook. "I am the shepherd," he announced to the commanding officer.

"Good. We've been waiting for you." He replied sternly. "I am Shaka, the Hadzian War Chief. I understand King Aku values you. I will do the same. We are to be briefed when the rumbles cease. Find a place to listen. All of you."

"Briefed?" Haven asked.

The Assemblage took their places behind the generals, who stood collected, discussing this or that. With a blaze of mightiness, one of them approached the seven. The Norse battalion's Jarl engaged them like a champion. He was a towering man built for war, resembling a grizzled gladiator. His hands were wide enough to crush a skull. His arms were thick, dirty, and scarred. A strong man with a convicted stare. A man who favored battle. His rough exterior matched his inner person—a strong leader of men. The struggles of his life built in him not an enjoyment of peace but the sufferings of war. He would not know what to do with peace if someone handed it to him.

His armor, covered in dirt and mess, spoke of victory and courage. Even his iron cap was one of intimidation. It sat heavy on his head. What looked like ram horns protruded from the sides. Whether it was for show or protection, it surely venerated power.

Initially, he spoke to the seven young men without tact: "You must be the children that old conjure sent here. I'm not sure why I'm given boys and not men." Noticing Epoch, he lightened his demeanor. "Whoa, look at this one." He appealed. "We've got a Giant over here!" He shouted to the other generals.

He then pulled a flask from behind his vest. "I am Gunnar, the Jarl to the Viking army. I hear mighty things about you seven." He drank from his flask and then looked over at the Giant. "You, the tall one. What is your name?"

Epoch lifted his head. "Epoch, son of Mammonthal."

"Can you wield a sword and shield?" Gunnar asked. Epoch nodded, so Gunnar gave him his order. "Stay by my side. I will equip you as a berserker within the inner circle of my battalion. I need tall men."

Unable to control his adornment for the Jarl, Sven stepped forward. "What about me, sir? I'm ready to fight, too." His squeaky voice did not help his case.

Gunnar looked down at him. His eyebrow curled as he held back a snicker. "And who are you, wee one?"

"I am Sven, the seventh son of Gorl, the West Lud Hunter," he announced in a much deeper tone than before.

"Gorl?" Gunnar grinned. "Fine warrior. As are his sons. But this is the first I hear of you, Sven."

Understandably, Sven grew nervous, his eyes moving from side to side. "It won't be the last either, sir. I'm a fine fighter," he insisted.

"But your father did not enlist you. Are you the runt of his litter?" Gunnar asked menacingly. Haven stepped forward to challenge the Jarl, but Sven stepped further. Gunnar grinned, towering over both of them. Pleased with this confrontation, he looked down at Sven. "How does a wee one survive such a dangerous climb? You're so small."

Sven grinned, familiar with this type of demeaning intimidation. He knew this tactic well, belittled by his older brothers before. He knew exactly how to reply: "The same way those lice made it to the top of your filthy scalp." Sven jeered back.

His bold insult shocked his six comrades. Their jaws dropped.

Gunnar leaned back and belted out a laugh. "Good answer, wee one! Humor is a cunning shield. Your words are welcome at such a critical hour."

Sven grinned while his six comrades sighed, looking at one another with relief.

"Only a brave and relentless man can survive the journey you have made. And you remain able to fight!" Gunnar noted. "You are small, but your determination is not. You will fight beside your Viking brothers."

"Thank you, sir," Sven said, overwhelmed with happiness.

Gunnar gave one more piece of advice: "Sven, son of Gorl, your size will add a unique trait to this fight—one we do not yet have. May it serve you well."

The Assemblage looked upon their friend with admiration —especially Lunar, who pumped his fist. Sven looked at his friends, his eyes wide with excitement. He could not contain his excitement. "I'm a Drang!"

The other generals called for Gunnar's return. One of them shouted to him, "Gunnar, the Lion is ready to speak!"

This mysterious title caught the seven's attention, especially Haven's. He raised his head, looking for the reputable stranger Jehu had mentioned before.

Haven leaned into Bluff. "The Lion?" he whispered with a raised pitch. "I must speak with him."

Bluff nodded. "You must. He is a mastermind," He replied, his voice barely above a whisper. His eyes gave a piercing stare.

"How do you know this?" Haven said to him with eyes wide.

Bluff leaned in closer. "I saw him before you arrived. He lives below with the Dritts in a workshop full of potions. He claims to know how to destroy Snarlag."

Under the stone amphitheater of the Breathing Summit, a commencement unfolded. Shaka, Gunnar, and the three other military generals, each a pillar of their kingdom, abruptly turned and presented a unified salute to a figure emerging from a carved doorway in the rock wall.

The Lion received their full attention through the thick mist with a fearless saunter and quiet authority. Standing behind the generals, the seven strained their eyes to see him.

Captivated, Haven waved the fog away from his face, desperately trying to see him. He felt an inexplicable pull toward this sauntering stranger, a visceral connection that stirred a profound sense of wonderment within him, a feeling he had never experienced before. It was as if the stranger held the key to a world Haven had only dreamed of.

Walking with dauntless leisure and paying no mind to the mighty men who saluted him, the Lion stepped onto a smooth, stone platform. His tall but lanky frame revealed old age, as did the white hairs peppering his thick red beard and unkempt hair. They contrasted starkly against the pristine white of his clean, long coat. The spectacles perched on his nose caught the elusive sunlight, lending him an air of Geezer-like distinction.

All rumbling ceased, and a chilling silence fell over the mountaintop. He coughed into his fisted hand. He then lifted his head and peered out at those awaiting his words. "This is the calm before the storm," he said, his voice articulate and deep. "The animal's hibernation is complete. I have measured its breathing long enough. The animal will awake at any moment. Ready your men for war. And bring me the young shepherd named Haven."

The words hung in the air with a sense of impending doom. The five generals readily turned to join their armies. Shaka passed by them and tapped Haven on the shoulder. "Time for you to see the alchemist."

Haven's heart beat fast. Staring directly at the Lion, he decided promptly. "Time to meet this notorious one." But before Haven could approach, a sudden force violently shook the ground. The Assemblage fell into one another.

With a raised hand and madness in his voice, the Lion shouted across the rumbling. "It's awake! The animal is awake! It's awake!"

~ ~ ~

The summit shook, and pandemonium erupted among the five generals who raced toward their respective encampments. Haven struggled to remain upright. The ground convulsed beneath him, each jolt sending shockwaves through his legs. He planted his feet wide, his arms flailing as he kept his balance.

He returned his attention to the Lion, who he could no longer find. Torn between his loyalty to the Assemblage and meeting the one he promised Jehu he'd find, Haven's mind raced. He was sure the Lion was the linchpin in all this. A man he was certain knew the answers he searched for. *How do I kill Snarlag? Why was I chosen?*

Snarlag's awakening rattled the mountain to its core. The Assemblage stood their ground, but a sudden rupture tore through the earth, creating a gaping chasm that threatened to devour them. With a desperate leap, Haven narrowly avoided the abyss; a hand that seized him just in time halted his fall. The Lion yanked Haven back from the edge, averting his probable death.

With a firm grip, the Lion pulled Haven from the edge of the gaping chasm onto stable ground. "Haven, follow me," the Lion urged, his voice carrying a tone of command.

Following him and seeking refuge near a rock wall, Haven had to know. "How do you know who I am?" he blurted out.

The Lion's gaze bore into Haven's, a glimmer of recognition shining through his spectacles as he replied, "I know many things which I will tell you! But first, you must destroy this animal!"

Watching this man's demeanor and hearing him speak, Haven's sense of connection to him increased. "But I don't know how to destroy it!" he exclaimed. "Why was I chosen to do it?" He was desperate for answers as the clashing of collapse surrounded them.

From across the widening chasm, the Assemblage called out to him. They looked unsure, caught between the beginning battle and Haven's precarious position. Seizing the fleeting moment, Haven cupped his hands around his mouth and shouted back with a fierce urgency that cut through the tumult of the quake.

"Find your people! Find your fathers!" he yelled across the chasm. "Fight beside them!" His voice carried not just a command but a plea, imbuing his comrades with a sense of duty amid the shaking.

"What about you?" Bluff called out to him.

"What about me?" Haven muttered to himself. He turned to the Lion, looking for an answer. "Yeah, what about me?"

"You have an animal to destroy," the Lion said assuredly as he turned to face him.

"Right." Haven agreed. He turned back to Bluff. "I'm going to kill Snarlag!" he shouted, unconvinced.

Bluff shrugged his shoulders, not convinced. The others fled to find their fathers. Bluff found himself alone there, waiting on Haven.

"Go!" Haven shouted at him. "I'll be fine! Just go!"

Pulling Haven back from falling rocks, the Lion knew time was short. "Do you have your necklace?" he asked him desperately.

The question caught Haven like a trap. His mind and expression went blank. He placed his hand over where it rested beneath his armor and clothing. "How do you know about my necklace?" he quavered.

"It will destroy Snarlag," the Lion replied with unwavering confidence. "Show it to me."

Haven placed both hands over his chest. He stepped back, fearing the man. "But how do you know about it?"

Blaring war horns erupted in the distance. War chants carried across the mountaintop, as did the marching of many soldiers. But Haven heard none of it. His only concern was with this new, meaningful figure in his life.

"Who are you?" Haven asked, tempering his angered fear.

"I will answer your questions when we have the time," he replied without patience. "Follow me. We've prepared a place where you can destroy Snarlag."

The Lion dashed into a carved doorway with a determined stride, disappearing into the depths of an underground passage. Haven followed him, his footsteps echoing down the winding hallway that descended into a hidden maze of hallways below.

He hurried behind this red-bearded man, calling out to him for answers. He repeated the same question: "Who are you?"

He fretted with each passing second, wiping sweat from his forehead. As dust fell from the ceiling, a knot of nervousness tightened in his chest. *Can I trust him? Will this hallway hold together?*

Another long hallway stretched before them, its walls adorned with faded murals of times past. Lanterns of fire lit up the path ahead. Haven's pace quickened as he followed the Lion's lead. "Who are you?" he asked again.

The Lion remained quiet in his quick pace. Haven's steps were swift but cautious. He hesitated to catch up with the older man. His eyes darted to the ceiling, his expression tense with the fear of imminent collapse. Clumps of dirt fell on his face. He kept his head down, brushing the dirt from his eyes.

At last, they reached the end of the hallway; it opened to a chamber bathed in a soft light from unseen sources. Haven's eyes searched the Lion's face for answers, his heart pounding with unbearable agitation. "Tell me now, who are you?"

In a moment of disclosure, the Lion lifted a necklace from beneath his own shirt. It held a pendant identical to Haven's, albeit in a striking shade of blue. The pendant twinkled, catching the glowing light of the chamber. Inside it was a tiny capsule, just like Haven's.

"You know who I am," the Lion replied, his grizzled voice carrying familiarity.

Haven's eyes widened in astonishment. The shared pendants, the cryptic words, and this indescribable connection to this man all pointed to a truth that had eluded him until now.

Haven gave in to the newfound understanding. His face relaxed, as did his shoulders. The two connected in the moment. Lowering his head, lost in the realization, Haven replied. "Yes, I know you."

18

THE BATTLE BEGINS

The battle began with immediate intensity. Snarlag rose from the den she had slept in for millennia. The encamped armies contended with her thousands of roots, which shot out from seemingly everywhere.

Each kingdom used its specialized skills. The Pulverans had their Refractionists, who shuffled into position as the head of Snarlag rose to the surface. They were a brilliant squad who dealt with light and mirrors—an artful and destructive tool. With their strategic positioning, they aimed their weapons directly at her.

Perched atop a ledge overlooking the summit's floor, they intercepted a beam of light piercing the skies above. They bounced it off a series of mirrors with deft precision, amplifying its power. Like a searing laser, the beam hurtled toward the creature. It blasted the very top of her head with blistering force—a direct hit!

Snarlag responded by shrieking a terrible sound. All those around the summit covered their ears. In her panic, her roots swung uncontrollably.

The general of the Pulveran army, Conroy Hugoh, lifted his head, still cupping his ears, and watched the enemy's appendages shake violently. Her roots flung up at the glass weapons. She shattered them, tossing many Refractionists into the air and destroying the ledge they had stationed themselves on. As her shrieking ceased, a snarl rumbled from the depths of her den.

Conroy stood firm, his bravery shining through. "Ready yourselves!" he shouted to his soldiers as shattered glass rained down upon them. He was a daring man, one even Gunnar, the Viking Jarl, respected. But this rising, fear-inspiring sight of the vermian creature crippled his hope for victory. Snarlag emerged from her lair. She peered down at him and his soldiers. They trembled, understanding this moment to be their last.

"This is no worm," he muttered, unable to comprehend her size.

Snarlag's appearance was frightening. Her enormity and horrifying visage loomed before him. She was not what they expected to find. Their nightmares couldn't concoct such a force.

Ridges marked the crown of her head down to her eyebrows. A pair of curling horns above her ears spread out like that of a ram. Her incredible height ascended as she slithered onto the surface. At the top of her snout and below her eyes, white tusks hung like that of an elephant. They stuck out with the length of six men. Her monstrous form dwarfed everything around her.

Her skin was wrinkled and cracked from age, and she had long, bristled hair. Each strand protruded from her snout and long neck, urticating from her body like a tarantula.

Conroy's gaze shifted to his soldiers, who stood frozen in fear. The men and women under his command stood behind him, synchronized in an attack posture. Fitted in gold and silver armor and equipped with white helmets and black eyewear, they lowered their crystal swords. Conroy gritted his teeth and understood their fear of death. He shouted what he figured to be his last command.

"Soldiers of Pulver! Do not cower at her height, but show her yours! Stand tall!" He turned back to behold the sight of the colossal beast. "For your children's futures! Charge!" he commanded, charging forward in his silver graphene uniform.

Every Pulveran soldier followed him. Their swords lit up like the daylight. Rays of light shot out toward Snarlag. The intense flashes blinded her. She closed her eyes and turned away, again shrieking a terrible sound. Conroy sprang toward her, screaming out his fears and dreams. But the soldier's crystal swords were no match for her tough skin.

Though piercing her, their attacks were irrelevant. Like that of a paper cut, she found them only irritating. Using her roots, she swatted them, scattering them in many directions. Those who snuck past survived long enough to pierce her again and again. They tried to do as much damage as they could. But their death came soon after. She quickly slithered over them, moving forward toward the Tribesman.

Lunar rushed to the battlefield only to step back when seeing the creature. He lost his breath, witnessing the tragedy. Snarlag slithered over his people with ease. He cried out for them. His voice quickly gave out, overtaken by the catastrophe.

Never could he imagine such a frightful sight. He whimpered as his legs gave out. He fell to the ground, mortified. "What am I to do?" He whispered to himself.

Though the Pulveran army's attack ended in destruction, it gave the Tribesmen time to arm their tall metal horns. Their general, Odyssey Amare, challenged his men to resist fear. They all watched as Snarlag's body slithered toward them. Their hands shook, and they struggled to breathe, unable to blow into their instruments.

With a raised fist, Odyssey Amare stood before them. "Tribesman, we are not cowards! Reclaim your hearts and find courage! Do not fail this order! Ready your lungs!" He ran behind their many horns and shouted his command, "Inhale! Blare!"

The Tribesmen blew into their brass instruments, and a deep sound vibrated across the summit floor. The sound reached Snarlag quickly, and its frequency took hold of her, lifting her long body off the ground.

Stunned by the sound wave, she floated there. The vibration held her in the air, levitating her above the ground. She couldn't make sense of it. The vibration proved powerful.

The Tribesman blew their horns as long as they could. Their breath gave out, ending their jarring sound. Snarlag dropped, landing hard, with the impact of a thousand boulders. It shook the summit into further collapse.

Given her vulnerable state, the Paleland Knights, revered as the stalwart guardians of the Paleland kingdom, launched their catapults and crossbows, which dripped poison and blazed with flames. Next were their cannons.

"Fire!" the commanding knight shouted. The cannon balls shot out directly at her. They, too, dripped with the poison. They designed some as explosives, and they detonated against her tough skin. She suffered mere bruises and scrapes.

She regained her composure and threw her roots at the frequency weapons before the Tribesman could use them again. Her boldness flattened the Tribesmen with little effort. Odyssey ordered the remaining few to retreat as if there were a place of safety to run to.

As they fled, she shook and cracked the ground beneath them, and with one mighty swoop, she destroyed each one. Only Odyssey Amare survived the attack. He looked to the knights, who contended with her cobweb of roots. He then looked to the Hadzians, who coordinated into formations eager to volley their arrows. "With all your might!" he yelled through his pain.

The Hadzian archers fired several rounds of arrows at the enemy. Most were lit with fire and poison. Snarlag lit up with intense heat, and the poison trickled down her like water down a spout.

The Hadzian war chief, Shaka, yelled to his archers, "Fire every arrow you have!"

Some aimed at her neck, others at her head, but only a few of their arrows stuck into her solid body. She snarled, noticing their persistence. She lifted a sizable root from below. The collapsing rocky floor swallowed a great deal of them.

Shaka rescued two of his men, carrying them away from the fray. They fled onto higher ground. "We cannot defeat this evil," he panted, eyes wide. He looked out to where he stationed his many archers. All were gone. In place was nothing but broken ground. He fell to the rock below, his armor heavy and taxing. Sweat stung his eyes, and while his anger boiled, his retaliation vented with mere seething words. "You cruel beast!"

He lifted himself just enough to draw his bow and aim at her. With precision, he released an arrow, its flight quick and accurate toward its target. However, Snarlag, ever vigilant, deflected it. Despite this, he continued to draw his bow again.

All the while, the warriors of the Norse lands busied themselves with their axe-throwing. They charged Snarlag, chucking sharp curved-bladed axes at her. The blades were so strong that they found success penetrating her skin, as did their spears. As they ran across the cracking summit floor, they cut many of her roots that sprang toward them. These Norse warriors were the strongest of all soldiers.

Gunnar rushed upon her body, careful not to pierce himself into her long, bristled hairs. He pulled his hatchets from his belt and lifted them above his head. He stabbed them directly into her side, pulling them down as much as his strength would give. He left two long lines of open flesh. So he pulled his giant berserker axe from behind his back, swung, and stabbed it into both creases of loose flesh.

"Feel my blade!" he yelled. She fretted, feeling the sting. For once, the poison reached her deeper flesh. Gunnar spit at it, enraged.

Sven ran onto the summit floor, readying his axe and shield. He was ready to join the fight. Looking for his father, he caught sight of his hero, Gunnar, the champion of the Vikings.

As he raced to join him, he watched the terrible unfold. Snarlag lifted a root from behind Gunnar and punctured it into his back. She pushed it right through his chest and tossed him aside. Just like that, the Jarl of the Viking army fell in battle. His last action of war, though brave, cost him his life.

"No!" Sven screamed, falling to his knees. The unbearable truth crushed his heart. He stood and charged forward with his axe and shield, ready to die beside his hero. Lunar stopped him, however, grabbing his legs and taking him to the ground.

"Let me go!" Sven demanded. But Lunar held on tightly to him. "Let me go!" Sven insisted.

"Don't fight me!" Lunar begged as he held onto Sven's legs.

Sven reached out with his axe. "It killed Gunnar! It killed him!" he cried, trying to stand up to charge her once more. Again, Lunar prevented him.

As Viking berserkers ran by, Lunar jumped on top of him. "She will kill you if you run to her!" Lunar countered.

Sven looked back at Lunar, his eyes dripping and his head shaking. "But she killed him! Let me die in battle alongside him!" he cried out. But Lunar proved resolute. He covered Sven as the ground shook and dirt fell upon them.

"You will avenge him, Sven. But not this way." His words were enough to settle Sven's vengeful rage.

Snarlag continued to destroy all the life she could find. Sven sat up. Tears dripped down his cheeks. "She killed him, Lunar."

"I know," he replied, his eyes also filled with tears. "She took my people, too, Sven. There has to be a better way of fighting her. We must find Haven."

Sven believed this true, so they sprinted off together, leaping sinkholes and broken ground. They raced against the bedlam, their hearts pounding for revenge.

The battleground lay devastated by Snarlag's power. The might of her attacks dominated Wunduria's greatest armies. Murder was her achievement and purpose. In the wake of her anger, only a few survivors remained.

The Pulveran Refractionists were nearly all dead. General Conroy Hugoh dragged his surviving soldiers to safer locations. The Paleland Knights continued shooting their poisoned crossbows at their enemy but with little success. Though hundreds of her roots were severed, she had thousands more at her disposal.

The knights loaded a catapult with a heavy piece of blyer stone, pulled the restraining rope, and launched it. The projectile soared through the air at a rapid speed. It successfully hit Snarlag, this time between her eyes. It shattered to pieces and appeared to knock her senseless.

Many knights fell into a mountain crack. The heavy shaking enveloped the knight's war machines into the ground below them. Then they felt her deep snarls. Their bodies filled with vibration as the mountain consumed most of them.

Bluff and Epoch found Sven and Lunar. Together, they turned to witness the terror Snarlag unleashed. None of them could find their fathers, and fighting beside their people was no longer viable. They did not have time to mourn the dead.

"Where are Akimu and Ruddy?" Bluff asked, but the others didn't have an answer.

As the rockworm's assault slowed, fatigue weighed upon her. She was simply tired. Her movements labored as she heavily panted, drained from her mighty onslaught. In her ancient age, she dripped fluids from her eyes and mouth.

The four of them, keenly observing her dwindling energy, seized the opportunity to strategize.

"She's tired," Epoch noted.

"If someone can kill this thing, it will be Haven, right?" Lunar recalled. "We should be with him, then."

They all exchanged agreeable glances.

"Yes, this is our last chance. Let's go find him." Bluff agreed.

Uncloaking unexpectedly, Akimu appeared before them.

"Akimu!" the four exclaimed, pleasantly surprised.

Waving his hand, the Flame Shadow gestured for them to follow him. He darted off with incredible speed across the rocky terrain, his feet finding precarious purchase on the cracked and ruptured surface. With every stride, he maneuvered around gaping fissures and sharp outcrops.

Watching their Flame Shadow comrade dash along the fragmented landscape with ease, the four others watched with admiration. Trying to show themselves as agile, they ran together to find their leader.

The harsh truth of the army's defeat lay behind them as they departed. Despite the combined efforts of the Norse warriors, Snarlag proved to be too much for them.

With a thunderous roar, she lashed out. Her horned head swayed menacingly and decimated the Viking warriors with a single swipe of her massive tusks. Axes clattered, and the once-unyielding warriors were tossed like leaves into the sky, along with their brave resistance. The mountain air carried the screams of their valiant struggle. Few survived the decimation.

19

SNARLAG

"Yes, I know you," Haven replied, looking down, gripped by the Lion's true identity. Surrounded by the persistent shaking of the earth, Haven looked up and stared into the eyes of the man he understood to be his father, Daniel June.

Unsure how to respond, he readied his mind to leave the chamber and this newly revealed truth behind. He steeled his resolve, setting aside personal revelations for the urgency of their shared cause. He would not let his heart and emotions dictate his actions.

"How do I kill the worm?" he asked, his voice steady but edged with nervousness, trying to downplay the gravity of the truth.

Sensing Haven's apprehension, Daniel directed him toward a practical course of action. "Climb that ladder to the surface," he instructed, pointing to the chamber's corner. Then he tore the blue pendant from his necklace and fastened it onto Haven's green one, linking their keepsakes with a metallic click.

"Divided, these pendants are mere tokens of remembrance," he said, looking down at Haven. "But together, they will dissolve inside the belly of Snarlag, destroying her."

"This is why I was chosen to fight her?" Haven asked, staring at the pendants.

Daniel shook his head. "Any man can wield this weapon," he asserted, handing the clasped pendants to his son. "But only one can defeat the animal. Only you can destroy her."

Recalling his father's words imparted to him years earlier, Haven spoke with newfound understanding, "These pendants can heal, or they can injure."

Daniel placed his hand over Haven's, which held the clasped pendants. "When I missed you most, my son, this pendant rested over my heart and healed me."

He then took the pendants and placed the blue side on his chest, activating a blue glow. Then he put the other side over Haven's, which lit up green.

"How?" Haven asked, mesmerized by the activation.

Gripping the glowing pendants, he explained, "Once clasped together, they activate by the beating of our hearts. That is how I made them. They'll only injure if you intend them to. Your heart has power over them."

Lifting his eyes from the pendants, Haven looked into his father's and replied discerningly, "So I *can* tame an earthquake."

Daniel's face relaxed into a warm smile, accentuating the charm of his beard. Behind his glasses, the lines around his eyes crinkled, adding depth to his expression of joy. "Yes, my son. You certainly can."

Hearing the snarls of the great rockworm, they both turned toward the ladder. Haven ran to it, but before ascending, he paused momentarily at the base. He turned back to face his father, pride etched across his features. "I'll make you proud," he said, his voice wavering.

"You're the hero, my son. Save Wunduria!"

The chamber then convulsed intensely. Dust clouded the air as the walls fell apart, heralding imminent collapse. With no time to spare, Daniel shouted to him, "Quickly!"

Haven gripped the wooden rungs of the ladder and cast one last glance over his shoulder. In that fleeting moment, a myriad of emotions passed silently between them. His father's face, illuminated by the flickering faint light, bore an unspoken farewell. As the walls crumbled, Haven turned away, fearing he just lost his father for good.

Haven's hands gripped the rickety ladder as the rumbling grew louder beneath him. Dust and debris rained down from above as the walls of the hole shuddered and cracked. He climbed faster, his heart pounding, every muscle straining to reach the top before the ground gave way. With one final push, he hauled himself up onto the summit floor, rolling away just as a deafening crash sounded behind him.

Breathing hard, Haven turned back to where the ladder had been, only to find that the entire hole collapsed in on itself, leaving nothing but a jagged pit of rubble. The ladder was gone, and with it, any trace of the way he had come. For a moment, he just stared, the realization settling in that his father was trapped under there.

"Focus, Haven," he said, closing his eyes. He looked down at the filled hole. "Please be alive, father." A tear fell from his eye.

Out of duty and obligation, he centered his attention on his purpose. He turned to see his whereabouts. Tall crags loomed above him on either side. They cast stark shadows under the sun's harsh, foggy glare.

Stepping forward, he heard the sounds of battle in the distance. The rocks' enclosure suddenly frightened him. They seemed oppressive, and he imagined them closing in.

He saw many things resting on the ground. Slain bodies of soldiers, weapons, and many other supplies. His muscles tightened, and he covered his mouth.

The rumbling softened, and the wind's howling swept into the alley. He lifted the necklace from around his neck, staring at the shining blue and green pendants clasped together. *I must find Snarlag.*

A familiar voice shouted in the distance. Ruddy ran out from beyond the crag walls, exclaiming with relief, "Haven, there you are!"

"Ruddy?" Haven said, relieved to see him.

"I was hoping to find you here," he replied, wiping sweat from his brow. "I was told to look for you here."

"By who?"

"Akimu's people, the Flame Shadow," he explained. "They just appeared out of nowhere, pretty wild. They brought me to this discreet location and showed me all these ingredients they collected."

"Ingredients?"

"Remember all those plants I was keeping in jars?" Ruddy replied, walking forward.

"Those weeds?"

"Yeah," Ruddy answered, leading him to a pile of dried vegetation. "Well, Akimu's people did the same thing."

They stood before a large pile of dried vegetation. Haven stepped closer to it, sniffing the air. "Smells musty."

"We're gonna light it on fire. Once Snarlag sniffs it, she'll come this way. The Flame Shadow will make sure of it. You need to be here when she arrives."

"And then what?"

"And destroy her!" Ruddy replied with a raised voice. "Didn't the Lion tell you how to kill her?"

Haven nodded with a chuckle. "Yes. Do you know where the others are?"

"No, but Akimu should be bringin' em' here any moment," he replied, captivated by the pile of smelly greens and weeds. "I knew she'd like this stuff," he said, proud of himself.

Akimu sped into the alley, with the others trailing behind him.

"Akimu!" Ruddy shouted, pointing in his direction.

Haven waved them his way, gesturing they converge in a huddle.

"Good to find you alive, boys," Haven said with a rising grin. "How's the battle going?"

Epoch shook his head, catching his breath, "Terrible."

Bluff grabbed Haven's shoulder. "Snarlag is a killing machine."

"It's that bad?" Haven worried.

Lunar raised his hand. "She's not a worm, either."

"She's massive," Epoch added.

"She has these huge horns and tusks," Sven said animatedly, using his hands to mimic the appearance. "She's a—"

"A killing machine." Bluff panted.

Haven contorted his face in disbelief. "Horns and tusks?"

A distant growl interrupted them, so they tightened their huddle.

Noticing all eyes on him, Haven peered around at his comrades. He held up his necklace, showing them the clasped pendants that beamed warmly.

"I have a weapon that will destroy her. It will burst within her, destroying her from the inside."

Nods of approval passed among them. Bluff added, "Snarlag's tired, recalling the creature's vulnerability. We just saw her with our own eyes. She pants like a dog."

His words formed a strategy in their minds.

Haven's scattered thoughts rushed out with rapt attention: "Then keep her tired and lead her this way."

Pointing to the pile, he urged Ruddy, "That stuff will lure her here, right?"

Ruddy nodded. "Like a bear to honey."

"Then let's ignite it," he commanded. "All of you, work together and bring her to me." But a visible tension still gripped them. They exchanged uneasy glances and rubbed the backs of their necks, unsure of what to do next.

"What's wrong?" Haven asked them.

They tilted their heads, wondering how to express their fears.

"She's a monster," Epoch admitted.

"Haven," Bluff implored, with tense lines around his eyes. The corners of his mouth turned downward. "We just watched her kill hundreds of warriors with ease. We are broken by it."

Haven sighed, and his voice resonated with empathy. "I am sorry, my brothers. I wish I could change what your eyes have seen." He then stood tall. "But remember, we are here, where we set out to be. Look at one another," he urged them. "Look at where we stand. We were called for this. Fathers have died for their children, husbands for their wives. So take your stand up here in the clouds. We might be young, but we are not weak. We will finish what we started. Please, will you follow me?"

After closing his eyes, Bluff confirmed what he knew to be right. "Yes, I'll follow you."

"I will follow you." The rest said in unison.

Haven relaxed his posture and joked. "And have fun out there. I mean, we're eighteen. Do what you do best."

Sven shouted his approval, clapping his hands. "You heard him, boys. Have fun livin'; have fun dyin'!"

Akimu lit the pile of dried vegetation on fire with one of his daggers. It ignited instantly and then extinguished, leaving a trail of smoke that ascended into the sky.

"She'll be here soon," Ruddy concluded as he ran out of the alley with the others.

Watching them go, Haven's face wrinkled, smelling the burning, musty scent.

"It stinks," Bluff cringed.

Haven grabbed some ashes and rubbed them onto himself. "This better work."

The ground rumbled with severity. "She's ready for us," Haven implied, turning to Bluff. "You better get going."

"No, I'm staying here with you," he said with a decisive nod. "I'll fend off those roots of hers."

"Good idea," Haven responded appreciatively. "And Bluff, thank you for sticking by my side."

In the distance, Snarlag growled, but instead of feeling her dread, they looked at each other and recited the words their mentor once told them. "Men fight not for their survival but for the survival of others."

Keeping their balance on the rumbling ground, Haven and Bluff stood back to back, ready to contend with Snarlag's roots. "Get ready, my friend," Haven said.

~ ~ ~

Back on the battleground, Snarlag's anger returned. Dozens of the Flame Shadow fought her, all cloaked from sight. They swung fire daggers, leading her toward the scent of the burned vegetation. She caught the smell and hurried her pace toward it.

Lunar and Epoch watched her contend with the blurry nuisances. As the many Flame Shadows directed her their way, she snarled menacingly. She turned her head in their direction.

Lunar turned to his tall, dark friend and smiled. "You're darkness."

Epoch grinned. "You're lightness." They tilted their heads up at her. "Get ready to run away." Epoch sneered.

"It's what I do best." Lunar smiled.

Snarlag pursued them, leaving the Flame Shadow behind. Epoch and Lunar both turned around and ran toward the discreet location. She quickened her pursuit, gazing down at the contrast of Epoch and Lunar's skin colors. Through her ancient eyes, she saw a mesmerizing shadow beside a glow. Unable to distinguish them as individuals, she pursued them out of curiosity.

"Time to offer her a choice! Light or darkness!" Lunar shouted. They separated directions, Epoch to the right and Lunar to the left. This frustrated her so much that she responded with ambush, lifting her appendages from the soil to grab at the light.

With his radiance, Lunar sprinted through the quaking havoc. His luminous glow captivated her ancient sight. He dodged her roots as he fled with impressive speed and agility. His brilliance acted like a beacon against her evil. Unlike his people, who fought her with light beams, his soft skin's glow pleased her senses.

Unable to capture the glow, she swung her roots toward what she perceived to be a shadowy figure. Unafraid, Epoch punched through them. Her grasp for light failed, as did her desire for darkness. Epoch pressed forward. He was a relentless force against the creature's onslaught. He and Lunar led her far enough. It was now their comrade's turn to fight.

Sven, swift and agile, navigated the fragmented ground. The shaking rock floor was no match for his skill. He leaped over cracks and evaded falling rocks, fitting through the tiniest spaces. With excellent precision, he hurled his axe, piercing her face. Though it was a mere cut, she shook her head and snarled, perturbed by the sting. Sven's courageous act distracted her enough to allow the others to carry out their plans.

Lunar and Epoch rejoined side by side, sprinting toward the discreet location. Sighting the glow and shadow, Snarlag swatted at them, but they dodged her anxious reach.

She grew angrier. The precarious mountain terrain vibrated as she growled. That is when she smelled the fragrance of the smoke. Her mind raced, overwhelmed with too many senses. Her old age and centuries of slumber worked against her.

Young Ruddy, slick and untamed, saw his opportunity to attack. He slid down a rock hill on his shield and snuck into perfect position. With his sling in hand, he shot a pellet, and with perfect aim, he hit Snarlag in her right eye. She shrieked in panic.

She then felt a tickle up her back. She flinched and turned her head, blinking her damaged right eye repeatedly as it filled with tears. The shrewd Flame Shadow, concealed beneath his cloak, evaded the monster's notice. Invisible Akimu scaled the rockworm's colossal back and neck.

Just as the creature sensed danger, the cunning secret unveiled himself by igniting his fire daggers. With a calculated strike, he thrust both of them into her left eye, causing an anguished scream to travel through the crumbling mountain landscape. Quite injured and filled with hysteria, terror fell over her. Without consideration of where it would lead her, she moved closer to the enticing, musty scent.

There in the alley, resourceful Bluff brandished his red staff. With each skillful swing, his staff cut through the tangled mass of roots, carving a strategic path for Haven. He awaited Snarlag's entrance into the alley.

But at that moment, Snarlag lifted the largest of her roots through the grounds of the discreet location, crumbling the rock floor beneath them, sending both Haven and Bluff into her den below. A fury of many other things fell into the den along with them, including slain bodies and many supplies.

There, deep inside her lair, they struggled to stand. They could not see through all the clouds of dust. They could, however, hear their enemy's snarls. And they echoed as she slithered inside the lair. She sniffed the air again and again.

"Bluff!" Haven shouted, coughing heavily.

"Yeah! I'm here!" he responded. "You hurt?"

Haven felt his body and checked himself for injuries. "I don't think so."

Bluff responded with an immediate complaint. "Really? My whole body hurts! I think my ribs broke!"

"Well, yeah, me too," Haven agreed. "But I'm not dead."

"Oh, yeah, me neither!" Bluff responded in a more resounding tenor.

Snarlag lowered herself into her deep, cavernous lair as they busied themselves with reassurances; the two of them felt her presence. Haven found himself covered in more of the vegetation's ashes. *Come and get me.*

He looked to the ground around him and picked up a rope that had fallen inside with him. He tied the pendants at one end of it and wrapped the other end loosely around his arm.

The dust cleared enough for Bluff to see Snarlag slither onto the den floor. Using her roots as a harness, she guided herself inside.

Once on the floor, she slithered toward Haven slowly. She had picked up his scent.

With every bit of courage he had, Bluff stood between her and Haven. He held his red staff high above himself. As his tool of resistance, he pointed it toward her.

He stared her down as her damaged eyes squinted and dripped with bloody tears. Her massive tusks pointed out right at them, and her heavy horns hung at the sides of her head. She was as frightening as ever in the shadows of her lair. But Bluff took courage. "You will go no farther!" he shouted, holding out his red weapon. Haven looked on with admiration, watching his friend prove his bravery. He squinted, trying to see Snarlag clearer through the dust.

Using very little energy, she tossed Bluff aside with one of her roots. He disappeared into a dark corner. She snarled and slithered slowly toward Haven. He felt the vibration of her snarls in his chest. Stones and dirt fell onto him from the large hole above him. As he stepped back, he noticed a Norseman's helmet in the dirt beside his foot. He lifted it and recognized the ram horns that protruded from the sides. This was Gunnar's helmet. He placed it on his head, giving him a surge of courage. She moved closer, smelling the scent of Haven.

As the cloud of dust settled, he caught a glimpse of her. He froze in terror. Nothing could be more frightening to his eyes.

After beholding her, he gritted his teeth and pumped his fists, trying to find courage. "Open your mouth," he whispered as he watched her tower over him. He searched for where her mouth was, but he could not find it. *Does she even have a mouth?*

As she slithered closer, it became clear. She sniffed the air and salivated at his scent. He saw drool drip from a crease. Below her tusks, a separation occurred. Her mouth opened to reveal a great horror. Like the long bristled hair that covered her face, she showed her long, sharp teeth. Her tongue snuck through the tight creases between them. It forked at the end and flickered like that of a snake. A new fear overcame him as he watched her drool with hunger.

With her appendages, she lifted several injured soldiers' bodies from the ground and above Haven's head. She used their limp bodies like puppets. Pierced into their spines, they became her mouthpiece. She spoke with evil intent, showing herself to be much more than a wild animal.

"You are the one chosen to defeat me," the deep voices growled. "You will be my last meal before I cast this land into the sea for eternity." She flicked her tongue rapidly, looking down at Haven with hunger.

He struggled to breathe slowly, shocked she could speak using others' mouths. He closed his eyes, preparing to be eaten. With the pendants in his grasp, he would be the end of her.

He gained enough courage to speak. "Why all this destruction?" he asked her, shouting as loud as he could.

She growled deeply. "Age has conquered me, young one," she said nastily. "If I cannot live, neither will any man." She then tossed most of the bodies behind her into the dark corners of the pit. Still using just one body, she moved it closer to Haven. "I never cared for my natural purpose. Lifting land above the seas so life could live after my death. I think not."

"But that is the way of life," he replied through his gritted teeth.

"Not for me. I will pervert my nature. I will choose the opposite." She sneered, tossing the last body aside. She lowered her head, ready to consume him.

He looked up at her eyes. They dripped with blood and tears. Her tongue again flickered, this time nearly reaching his body. He readied himself for death, holding the pendants close to himself. He closed his eyes, ready to be eaten. But then something incredible happened. Something he had forgotten about entirely. Yes, something amazing.

A most meaningful sound rang from far above. The horns of Tortuga Nue blew a powerful note. Their sound rung down into the cavernous den. There, above the pit, up in the sky, Gamba Tru arrived with his armada of skyships.

Up above in the mist, he shouted to his fellow Buccaneers, "Battle stations!" He then shouted down to all who could hear. "Sorry for our lateness!"

With large chains, his flagship and another carried a large boulder. High above Snarlag, they readied their weapon. They released the chains and dropped the boulder down into the lair. With a pulverizing force, the boulder fell upon the crown of Snarlag's head. Her head sunk to the ground, unprepared for such power, and her tusks cracked in many places.

In complete shock, Haven jumped back, avoiding the crash. He looked above to find the armada of Buccaneer skyships descending through the clouds.

Jumping from a plank off the side of Gamba's ship, several Buccaneer fighters, including Gamba and his sister Glori, fell into the hollow pit.

Glori, the bravest of all women, descended without fear of the vermian creature. Both she and Gamba descended upon Snarlag's bruised head and struck swords into her softened, bruised flesh.

Anguished by the pain, Snarlag lifted her head, shaking violently. She opened her mouth, shrieking a sound no one had heard throughout all time.

More Buccaneers descended upon her. They flung a chain into her open mouth. With impressive speed and precision, they attached both sides of the chain to hooks that fell from the vessels far above. With enough pull, they kept Snarlag's mouth open.

With an unwavering resolve, Haven clutched the clasped pendants that had bonded himself and his father. Channeling the collective strength of all Wunduria's fallen soldiers, he swung the rope in a wide arc, ready to launch the attached pendants. The determined rage collected upon the summit by all those who fought the creature carried Haven's will. At last, he let go of the rope, attempting what he had been called to do from the start: tame an earthquake.

The moment seemed suspended as the gleaming green and blue pendants sailed through the air, aimed unerringly toward Snarlag. The creature's maw, agape from the exertion of battle and too tired to fight the pulling chain, became an unwitting target. Time unfroze as the pendants, glinting like ethereal projectiles, found their mark, disappearing into the depths of her mouth.

Expectation settled over Haven, and he held his breath for several heartbeats, awaiting the unknown consequence of this bold gambit. Would his father's prediction prove true? Would the pendants Daniel June made so long ago be the catalyst needed to destroy this creature?

From the edge of the pit above, Epoch, Akimu, Lunar, Ruddy, and Sven watched it unfold. Consumed by nervousness, they hoped for Haven's victory and survival.

Deep inside Snarlag's throat, the combined pendants transformed into destructive energy. In that intense moment, Haven vividly recalled his father's words, "You're the hero, my son."

A surge of victory filled his heart. He braced himself for the impending victory, a fusion of his ideals and father's guidance. And so it happened: detonation!

A brilliant explosion erupted inside Snarlag. The combined energy of the pendants unleashed a dazzling burst of light and force. The surroundings trembled in acknowledgment of the climax, and as the shockwave expanded, the beleaguered creature convulsed heavily. The triumphant blast crippled her. Snarlag's colossal form ripped apart into fragments that scattered across the beaten ground of her den. Haven watched in awe and exhaustion as she burst apart from within.

Her body fell to the ground in thousands of pieces. Haven covered his face, stepping backward. This victory was gruesome.

After the loud spectacle, a hush followed—and for a moment, complete silence. Snarlag's spilled guts littered the ground. Her head landed on the pit's floor, decapitated and defeated.

All those who survived the battle collected around the opening to the pit. And for all those inside, they walked out of the shadows into the light. Gamba sauntered toward Bluff, who stood in an injured chill, now out of the shadowy corner. They both looked at what remained of their enemy.

Staring at the rocky fragments of the creature, Bluff spoke calmly to his Buccaneer mentor. "What took you so long?"

"I got held up," Gamba replied, with bits of the creature's flesh clinging to his body.

The other five climbed down into the den and ran to Haven. Together, the seven hugged with a victorious spirit. They pulled one another in and gripped each other tightly, like friends, like brothers—each jubilant for one another's survival.

They stood together in front of Snarlag's head. Haven had the only thing left to say to the enemy of Wunduria. "Age did not conquer you. Men did." The Assemblage lifted their heads, proud of one another's courage and actions.

Glori, the savage female Buccaneer, walked past them, nudging Haven in the back. "Don't forget me, love." She chimed with a grin.

Haven turned to see her muscled figure walking away. "Oh, yes. Sorry! Yes, ma'am! You conquered her, too."

Gamba looked on with approval while his sister winked at him and chuckled. "He reminds me of you at that age," she said kindly.

"I'll take that as a compliment. He conquered what I could not," Gamba said with pride in his gaze.

"You still had your revenge, my brother." She replied, resting her head on his shoulder. "Father would be proud of you."

"He'd be proud of us both," he replied.

All those below climbed out of the den and onto the crippled surface. They stood above their enemy's grave, looking down into the pit, relieved by her death. Survivors of the battle joined them there. And a roar of victory continued for a good while.

Cheers resounded across the summit. Survivors exchanged handshakes with arms clasped and hugged tightly, knowing all those they loved far below were safe. The once-tense atmosphere gave way to a vibrant celebration as soldiers lifted their voices in triumph.

Some danced, waving their swords in wild celebration, while others raised their hands to the sky, shouting chants of survival. Even the sky above them cleared as gusts of wind swirled the mist away and any remnants of Snarlag's colorful breath. The sun cast a warm golden hue on everyone's elated faces, marking the end of a challenging yet victorious day.

Bluff and Haven hugged, thanking each other for sacrificing so much. Lunar and Sven engaged in playful banter. Despite their fatigue, their movements were light-hearted and energetic. With smiles, Epoch, Akimu, and Ruddy teased and jostled playfully. They removed their armor happily.

Gamba looked on graciously as Glori stood beside him, singing a family song of triumph.

Jehu lowered from Gamba's flagship to meet his young friends. He cried out passionately as he greeted them with tears of exaltation. All seven embraced and thanked him.

"You believed in us from the start!" Haven exclaimed, exchanging laughs of relief with the Geezer. Tears trickled down their faces.

Conroy Hugoh, Shaka, and several Paleland Knights were among the survivors. They joined the Buccaneers and remaining Norseman warriors in song, singing songs of victory.

Altogether, about fifty men reclaimed their hearts among the six battalions as their adrenaline still coursed from battle.

Daniel June limped out through the crowd of cheering faces. He suffered injuries but, more importantly, stayed alive. Haven caught sight of him. He ran to him immediately. Daniel opened his arms. As they met, Haven fell into them.

"You're alive!" he cried.

Their embrace gave witness to the persevering love between father and son.

"I love you, my son," he cried.

There, Haven felt shelter and solace as he buried his face in his father's chest, his breaths shaky with emotion. Tears of relief streamed down his cheeks.

"Thank you, Father."

20
RETURNING HOME

After their celebration, the survivors covered the dead with stones. A memorial convened under twilight, the survivors gathered to honor the fallen souls who had given their lives in the crucible of battle. Draped in tattered uniforms, each man looked up to the star-lit sky, hoping to find comfort, but there wasn't any in that black eternity above.

Jehu spoke aloud the names of all those they lost. Then he gave a eulogy. He cleared his throat and held back tears. "All those we lost, we will remember. They protected those they loved and those they did not know. To truly honor them, we must live lives worth dying for."

He lifted his head to the stars before concluding, "We stand in remembrance, bound by appreciation for their selfless acts. They died before their time so Wunduria can live on."

There, beside the battlefield of the summit, Haven looked over the marks left behind from the fray. The jagged cracks of the rockworms's merciless force marked a reminder that life depended on victory over evil. Haven cared not for battle but understood it.

Standing beside him, his father observed him, content to be by his son. He had much to tell Haven, but all in due time.

Before anyone could find sleep, a cold wind blew over them. The skyships floated in the night sky, anchored to the mountainside. The Moving Mountain lay quiet, motionless in the calm. Many reflected on all that transpired.

Haven's thoughts wandered somewhere he did not expect: the harsh reality of war faded away, and despite his exhaustion, a quiet resilience remained inside him.

He sat up from his resting spot and looked for his comrades. His six closest friends were there, surrounding him, all asleep. A warmness rose in his chest. They had laughed, fought, and wept together. They fulfilled their original vow to follow him to the end. They honored their quest to reach the summit. And because of that, he could tame the great earthquake. Their victory concluded the purpose of their Assemblage.

Upon this reflection, Haven understood that a man does not stand still but moves with the urgencies of life. He endures and becomes a necessity not for himself but for the greater sum. He decided that makes a man a hero. He concluded that many heroes, whether dead or alive, surrounded him. From that day forward, that summit would be called Hero Summit.

Before he drifted to sleep, he looked at his father, who lay asleep on a cot, injured and wrapped in bandages. Daniel June, too, was a hero. He became weak so others could become strong.

~ ~ ~

Morning came quickly. The survivors of the great battle left behind the summit. Lifted by ropes, they boarded the Buccaneer skyships one by one. Glori commanded the Armada to descend from the mountain peaks. It was time for everyone to return to their homes.

They soared over the lush and vibrant landscape below, inspecting the damage caused by the earthquakes. Cracks cascaded down the mountainside and fractured the landscape below. Massive fissures split open the ground and shifted, leaving a trail of destruction. The vermian creatures' fury left behind scars but failed to destroy the innocent civilians living below.

The seven young men rested mostly on the flagship under sails full of wind. As they reached their destinations, their goodbyes to one another were bittersweet. Especially for Bluff, who had little to return to. He parted ways with Haven with these farewell words: "Maybe I'll drift your way soon."

The most difficult of goodbyes for Haven concerned his father. At the entrance of the nocturnal Sceadwian Forest, they stood beneath the protective towering oaks. Daniel's eyes looked deep into his sons. They exchanged a final, lingering embrace.

"I am proud of you, Haven. Please remember that. Continue to be a refuge for those in need. Know this, my son, I love you. While I heal, stay you."

And so Daniel June disappeared into seclusion with the cloak-and-dagger ways of the Flame Shadow.

Tears welled in Haven's eyes, his heart heavy with the impending loss. After a strong embrace, Daniel withdrew, promising to return.

Upon Haven's arrival home, his sorrow faded when joy overcame him. A certain Wally Russ shouted from a distance, "Hello! Hello there!" Haven looked up to find the man riding Thunder toward his tree home.

"Thunder!" Haven exclaimed.

As soon as Wally Russ dismounted the stallion, it charged forward toward Haven, who greeted the horse with great affection.

"My friend, my friend! How are you, boy?" Haven exclaimed.

Wally laughed loudly, watching them reunite. "Good to see you again, young man!"

Too excited to reply, Haven mounted Thunder. Its tail swung wildly, and nostrils snorted many excited noises. They took off into a gallop, a galvanized demonstration of rekindled friendship. Haven and his trusted companion Thunder rode throughout the field and circled Wally Russ, who clapped, joining in on the fun. Even some of the sheep bounced with excitement.

As the days progressed, Haven returned to contentment, but this time he felt fulfilled. King Aku assigned him to work as a ranger after an extended leave from work. Haven agreed happily.

He and his mother discussed many things over lunch, but nothing regarding his quest to save Wunduria. Their conversations were new and different, as Haven had become a much different person. His ears were open to understanding with all those he conversed with, but he remained firm in his morals and convictions. Perspective was a good thing, but integrity was greater.

The royal family held a ceremony in the capital city to celebrate and honor those who fought for Wunduria's survival. Each kingdom followed suit in a location they chose. The celebratory day became known as Akaka Non, which, to the Hadzians, means protection.

There, in the city of Ekurh, all seven members of the Assemblage united to be honored. The celebration was indeed with the people of San Hadza. From one end of the city to the other, Hadzians carried on with jubilation.

Despite not wanting to, the seven wore costumes the leaders of their people had prepared for them. Each stood decorated with the styles of their cultures. They stood before a large audience, who cheered for them with songs of gratitude.

"We look ridiculous," Bluff said to his comrades, looking at his and the other's costumes.

Scanning their outfits, Lunar responded with his expected charm. "I think we look great. Plus, I've been working out. My muscles are showing."

Sven rolled his eyes. "No, they're not. You look scrawnier than ever."

"You look shorter," Lunar teased. Sven curled his lip but gave in to a gentle laugh.

Haven smirked, happy they were all together once again. He looked out at the crowd that cheered for them. Children of San Hadza pointed at Epoch, amazed by his size. Boys were impersonating the seven, pretending to be heroes fighting for survival.

Filled with pride, Diane waved at her son, who stood before the large crowd. He smiled and waved back at his gracious mother. He then looked around at those in attendance, trying to find familiar faces.

There, besides his mother, were King Mikel and Queen Sade Aku, who honored Haven and the other six with a ceremonial bow. The San Hadzian general Shaka and a few surviving Hadzian archers stood beside the Assemblage as part of the guests of honor. Jehu and Gamba were there as well, but instead of being among those honored, they sat with the Royal Family and showed respect to the honorees. Hidden in unknown places was the Shadow Flame, accompanied by Daniel June, who looked on with pride for his son.

"Look who's here!" Epoch said to his friends, pointing to a group of individuals in the crowd. The seven all looked and found Juxtus Lunder with his daughter Miley and a beautiful woman.

"Is that his wife?" Ruddy guessed.

Akimu shrugged his reply, which summed up the other's thoughts. This woman, Lindah, was younger than the old scoundrel, Juxtus. The seven would later learn that the pouch Jehu had given him at the pub contained a cure for her illness. It healed her well. She stood beside her husband and daughter, beaming with gratitude.

The crowds soon quieted down, watching King Aku walk before the seven young men, placing valor awards around their necks. The seven looked at their awards and then at one another. With enthusiasm, a sea of faces erupted into applause. Clad in costumes adorned with honors for valor, the young recipients of recognition stood humbled, their expressions a mix of gratitude and humility.

"This is amazing," Sven said proudly. He saw his parents out in the crowd cheering for him. His chest swelled with nobility.

"You've earned it," Lunar replied, patting his friend's back.

"We all have," Haven shouted to them as the crowd's loud cheers resonated. Above the seven was a banner that read, The Sons of Wunduria. Each one was considered family and a hero to all six kingdoms. And heroes they would need to be.

A great disturbance cut the celebration short. A sudden shock jolted the crowd into a frenzy. Pandemonium ensued as the once cheerful crowd scattered in shock at a sudden intrusion. A colossal animal crashed through several display tents. Gasps of surprise and screams filled the air, transforming the festive atmosphere into one of chaos and fear.

The seven watched a massive bear roar its way before them. This was no ordinary beast but something immense.

"Is that what I think it is?" Lunar gulped.

"It can't be," said Epoch, shaking his head.

But it was what they feared. The ancient myth, King Killer, stood before them, ready to feed.

"Oh, it is. King Killer is alive," Sven said, gritting his teeth.

Frantic shouts and hurried movements painted a scene of swift evacuation as the crowds struggled for safety. The giant bears's footsteps reverberated through the gathering, scattering people in all directions.

Once known only through anecdotal claims, the colossal bear King Killer existed as real as the people who escaped it. The animal stood on two legs with long claws extending from its powerful paws, and its eyes bore a fierce intensity, surveying the startled onlookers. It stood twice the height of Epoch. The beast's rhythmic breathing broke the silence that followed the initial shock.

Gamba Tru walked out to attack the creature, but Jehu pulled him back. "No, my friend. Looks like our heroes will handle this." Gamba turned and looked ahead of the creature to find the seven young men ready to subdue it. In that fraught moment, King Killer became an unexpected centerpiece of danger. They were prepared to contend with it and prove their place in legend and history as heroes ready for their call.

On top of his stallion, Haven called out to his six brothers, who stood behind him in a strategic chevron attack position. Their faces were adrenaline-fueled, standing before the roaring beast. With a shared nod, they armed themselves with their weapons. Except for Haven, who caught a sword Gamba tossed to him, and Ruddy, who snagged his sling from the hands of his sweet love, Kidty, who fell back into the waiting arms of Shumi and Emmy.

The glint of resolve in Haven's eyes reflected a collective decision to confront the unexpected threat head-on. As the enormous bear stood its ground, the seven prepared their hearts for battle. The clash between man and beast was inevitable, and in that charged moment, a new narrative unfolded—one of a continuing effort by these seven heroes to provide safety.

"Looks like we're back at it, men," Haven shouted to his brothers behind him. "You ready?"

Bluff, Akimu, Sven, Lunar, Ruddy, and Epoch shouted their reply, "We will follow you!" They readied their weapons as they locked eyes with the formidable beast. Resolve flashed across their faces. They were more than ready to fight this danger.

This giant bear fell to all fours and charged toward them. Haven lifted his sword and pulled on the reins of his loyal stallion, commanding his team of heroes.

"Sons of Wunduria, charge!"

SIX MONTHS LATER...

EPILOGUE

In the dull grey skies of the Palelands, leaders from the six kingdoms gathered in the Grand Hall Tower. There, besides the relentless sea, a discussion was in order.

Raindrops fell on the stones, a rhythmic cadence punctuating the air as the dignitaries gathered. The air hummed with anticipation, their meeting a response to the looming concerns of an unforeseen menace. Each leader had much to inform the others about.

Queen Ialdya took her place beside a wide, circular table. Her diplomate and the leader of the Paleland Knights joined her. She surveyed the others who joined her there: King Aku and his War Chief, Shaka; the Prime Minister of Pulver, Lady Freya, and her Military General, Conroy Hugoh; Several Tribesman Emissaries; King Amund of the Norse Isles and two of their Magnates stood tall; and Gamba Tru of the Buccaneers with his sister, Glori. Jehu the Geezer stood beside him.

A hush fell on the greetings between parties as heavy doors swung open, revealing the entrance of a venerable sage draped in robes that whispered tales of ancient wisdom. It was the greatest of Geezers, Lorcan. Wrapped in regal azure, the fabric bore intricate golden embroidery, mirroring the constellations in a night sky. All respected Lorcan's presence. A crown of silver adorned with symbols of knowledge rested upon his head.

The Grand Geezer settled upon the troubled gathered leaders like a lantern in the mist. With a nod, he signaled the commencement of discussions. His thin lips opened slowly.

"I, Lorcan, am proud to meet with you all. We are months removed from the battle with the vermian beast, yet a new disturbance threatens our land. Each of us must share our reports. May we begin with the Tribesman?"

One of the Tribesman Emissaries, his face covered with disdain, abruptly emptied a sack onto the surface of the grand table. Rotted vegetation poured out of it. The pungent odor wafted through the hall, eliciting wrinkled noses among the gathered leaders. With palpable disgust, the emissary spoke of crops that withered into wastelands, his voice carrying the weight of frustration and desperation.

And so each shared their stories of failing crops, fruitless lands, and vanishing forests—a rate of infection and death none had seen before. But when the time for Gamba Tru to speak arrived, all grew even more concerned.

The vindicated Buccaneer leader spoke with authority. His eyes were wide with trepidation. In a calm tone, he recounted unsettling reports from the outskirts of his islands—such as unexplainable creatures and sounds throughout the night.

"Strangeness is lurking about," he said in a disturbed tone.

"I believe his reports," King Aku added. "San Hadza can attest to such sights. We caught aggressive animals we had never encountered before. Is it new life, or are things changing?"

Jehu joined in the discussion, walking toward Lorcan, his fellow Geezer. "Snarlag's death preserved our lives, but it has come at a cost. Though dead, her roots still lay below our lands, decaying. I believe they are poisoning the soil, causing our crops and forests to die. I was there when she tapped into the mind and voice of Bron Crowl. She told me her death would bring consequences. I fear she's right."

"And what of these creatures?" King Amund of the Norse Isles questioned.

"That remains a mystery," answered Jehu.

EPILOGUE

As the evening continued, the leaders of the six kingdoms recounted stories of unknown creatures and violent men, acknowledging a common threat. Hostility and unnaturalness were consuming life on their land. Women were forsaking their natural selves.

Those at the table looked at each other warily, without trust. Even they were changing. Something debauched was happening, and they did not understand how to stop it.

High above, concealed on the grand hall's highest window ledge, a hidden figure observed the unfolding talks with a sinister smirk. In the shadows, this clandestine manipulator reveled in the confusion that rippled through the great hall below.

Unbeknownst to Wunduria's leaders, this hidden figure held the strings of discord, orchestrating the unsettling reports that fueled their fears. He was the architect of their worries, a puppeteer weaving a web of deception and darkness. This secret creator of turmoil was the very one they had once trusted: Daniel June.

TABLE OF CONTENTS

ABOUT THE AUTHOR

Joshua Allen is an imaginative storyteller and dedicated adventurer from Western New York State. Growing up surrounded by city and country living, Joshua developed a deep love for fantasy, often dreaming up heroic quests and oddball characters.

He spent much of his life as a musician and kept his writing merely a hobby. His passion for storytelling finally ignited in his thirties as he began to take his writing much more seriously. Like most fantasy writers, he finds inspiration from Tolkien's writings and the story of Peter Pan.

Sons of Wunduria, his debut novel, has garnered acclaim for its vivid world-building and dynamic characters. Joshua Allen enjoys traveling and learning about our incredible earth in his spare time. He has an affinity for animals and creation.

Currently residing in Rochester, New York, Joshua Allen is working hard on the next thrilling installment of the Sons of Wunduria series. Connect with Joshua Allen on social media to keep updated with his growing world of Wunduria.

Made in United States
North Haven, CT
02 December 2024

60737204R00127